4|16|13
$8.99
I

4|13

Withdrawn

Love Lett

By

Bryan Mooney

A Novel

D0000661

L

Books by Bryan Mooney

LOVE LETTERS

A SECOND CHANCE

THE POTUS PAPERS

These books by Bryan Mooney are available wherever fine books are sold.

This novel is dedicated to Bonnie, my wonderful, loving wife.
Thank you.

Acknowledgements

I would like to thank all of those individuals who helped me along the way to the final completion of this novel, particularly my "special advisors & readers," which include Cindy Goetzinger, Judy Hanses, Carol Kayne, Michael Naver but especially my loving wife Bonnie, my toughest critic. Their guiding hands and direction kept this ship on its proper chosen course and their insights, patience and encouragement throughout the process were invaluable.

Also, this novel would not be possible without the incredible talents of my extremely versatile editor, Eliza Knight.

I can't thank all of you enough. Thank you.

- BDM

"My Dearest Darling," the love letters began, and try as she might, she could not stop reading the letters she found in the old books. After reading one she was compelled to reach for another. Her curiosity urged her on. She could not stop...

If *you* found a love letter in an old book, would you read it?

Suppose you purchased some books from a bookseller at a flea market and upon returning home discovered love letters inside, what would you do? Would you read the letters? Would you try to return them? Would you destroy them?

That is the dilemma that Katie Kosgrove finds herself in when she discovers love letters written by the man she knows only as Jack. Curious but unable to locate him to return the love letters, she begins to read.

The letters all began with the same greeting, "My Dearest Darling," and end with, "Forever Jack". The letters transform her life in ways that she never would have imagined. She is thankful to the handsome stranger she met only once.

Katie knows exactly what she would say to him if she were to ever see him again, until one day he reappears, back in her life. Their world begins to change once more, but the letters have an awesome power over both of them, until...

Chapter One

Katherine Kosgrove locked the front door of her secondhand bookstore and pushed the large boxes of books over to the old green sofa in front of the fireplace. She made herself comfortable sitting back with a large glass of wine, with her favorite music playing softly in the background and her cat Felix snuggling beside her. Katie had saved Felix from certain destruction at an animal shelter in Boca Raton. Apparently nobody else wanted a one eyed cat but he was her buddy. Independent as hell, like her, but her buddy nonetheless.

Even though it was late, she began to search through the boxes of books she purchased at the flea market that day. She needed to catalog her new purchases for tomorrow. Felix purred for more food but soon dozed off to sleep. Katie had to be ready for her early Monday morning customers, who would be eager to search through any new books she placed on her "Just Arrived" rack.

While sorting through the first box, she could not help but be reminded of the ruggedly handsome doctor at the flea market who sold them to her. He said his name was Jack and that he was downsizing to a smaller house because his wife recently passed away. He told her the books belonged to his wife.

The used bookstore, aptly named "Second Hand Rose," was housed in a former two-story general store. The downstairs main floor was her bookstore and the second floor was her apartment. The place had tons of space and the rent was cheap, perfect for her purposes. At the rear of the store was a rustic old stone fireplace. Katie made this area cozy and inviting for her customers. Bookshelves lined the walls and a sofa faced the working fireplace. It wasn't just pretty, it was functional as well.

Katie's customers could peruse the books they were considering or wait out any of the frequent Florida rainstorms in front of the of its warm glow, drinking her freshly brewed Orange Indian Tea.

She sometimes lit the fire during the rare, cool Florida winter days when the temperature dropped into the chilly range. Sitting there on the sofa she smelled the faint woodsy smoke from the last time the flames burned the old logs on the steel grate. But most of all, Katie enjoyed the stack of white birch logs she usually left on the open grate. They reminded her of home and the sofa made an inviting and comfy place to curl up with a good book.

She sorted through the first box, taking them out and arranging them by category, condition and genre. The first box was mainly romance novels, which were her customers' favorites. She found paperbacks written by authors such as Jackie Steil, Robin Macy, Maureen Hare and Francesca Delarina among countless others.

There was poetry books by Keats, Browning, Frost and a hardback book of poetry by an unfamiliar poet named Allison White, which she found buried in the bottom of the box. She placed it in her own personal "To Be Read" pile.

Katie started forming other piles and was nearly done with the first box, when she found the classic, *Rebecca,* by Daphne Du Maurier, the twisted classic love story her mother enjoyed reading. Her mother loved it so much she had wanted to name her either Rebecca or Daphne, but Katie's father would have none of it. Her mom lost that battle and she was named Katherine, after her paternal grandmother.

Her mother, the ballet dancer Roberta Casina, grew up outside the town of Big Sky, Wyoming on a large cattle ranch and would spend any of her idle time reading. Katie went back to the ranch many times with her mother when her parents fought. She loved its wide open spaces and undisturbed view of the heavenly stars. The ranch was sold at her father's insistence when he ran into financial troubles. Her mother never said a word about it but Katie always knew she resented the loss. The last time she was there was to scatter her mother's ashes across the wildflower fields near the ranch.

Next she came across her favorite, *Wuthering Heights* by Charlotte Bronte. "Heathcliff," she murmured out loud, her voice emulating the tone of the novel. "Heathcliff," she sighed again, an impassioned memory, causing Felix to raise his sleepy head and glance at her.

"Go back to sleep," she said to her feline fur ball, caressing his forehead. "Back, back to sleep, back to sleep," she soothed and he was soon purring again, dreaming whatever it was that cats dreamt.

Her mind wandered back to the man at the flea market. He reminded her of some Hollywood movie star, rugged good looks, tall, broad shoulders and an easy smile. He was the type you would recognize in an instant but could not place his name.

She glanced through the classic and even though she'd read it countless times she always found the immortal love story mesmerizing. She smiled to herself, holding the cherished book in her hand. *Jack's wife had very good taste,* she thought, tossing it onto her growing personal "To Be Read" pile.

The book bounced off the sofa and landed on the floor, spilling out what appeared to be a handwritten note onto the carpet in front of her. Katie reached for the piece of paper lying on the floor.

She unfolded the blue lined note paper and read the first line of the letter, *My Dearest Darling*.

Katie's eyes widened. *Whoa. Oh my god, this is a treat and a treasure. And most women don't get to read love letters and far fewer have love letters written to them. Most men have trouble writing and remembering a grocery list. But what do we have here?*

She clutched the letter tightly to her chest, looking around to see if anyone saw her reading someone else's love letter. It was a reflex reaction. *Of course there's no one here. It's one a.m. Just Felix and me.* She had to know more.

Katie glanced at the blue paper. This could be a very private letter but she could not resist reading on. Her curiosity got the better of her, as Felix yawned in his sleep. "I know, I know what curiosity has done to cats," she whispered, then she began to read.

March, 2007

My Dearest Darling;

I saw a sunset today, a beautiful sunset. It reminded me of you and of us. Do you recall how we would measure our days by the sunsets we saw? We would always take the time to stop and watch them, no matter where we were.

Remember the orange and red sunset over the plains of the Serengeti—we held hands like school kids and drew each other close, hearing the lions roar just beyond our fires. Remember the awe inspiring sunset on the Greek island of Syros? Do you recall the marvelous sunset from the top of the hills overlooking Molokai? Oh, that magical Hawaiian island, shrouded in rainbows every day, from the wondrous mornings until the cool nightfall. And remember the sunrises on the beach in Panama? But the ones I recall most fondly were the morning sunrises on the beach of Islamorada in the Keys. It was always enough to take my breath away, as long as I was there with you, my love.

Breathtaking! The simple silent beauty, there is nothing on earth like it and to spend it with you was like gold.

My favorite sunset of all time was on our cruise and we were dining on board, sailing the blue green waters of the Caribbean. From our window table we could faintly see the soft yellow rays of the setting sun. Together we grabbed our champagne glasses and left our dinner to be alone. We watched the most gorgeous sunset of all. I cherish times such as those, my love.

Every time I see a sunset, I think of you and remember your beauty and what you mean to me. Each sunrise and sunset brings us closer together. Which sunsets do you recall as your favorite? Which sunrises do you cherish? I count the sunsets until we are together again.

I love you and miss you.

Forever,

Jack

"Wow..., how romantic can you get?" Katie took a large, loud, gulp of wine. The letter was signed simply, *Jack*. No last name. It had to be the same good looking Jack she bought the books from. He must have written these letters to his wife.

That was some letter. Jack and his *Dearest Darling* really cared for one another other. Then Katie remembered he'd told her his wife died a while back.

This fellow Jack, he really loved her. He knew what his wife wanted. She wanted what every woman wants. *Simple really*, Katie thought, *we want love and happiness, coupled with trust and respect. Everything else is just fluff. Nothing else matters.*

She gazed at the hand written letter she held in her hand. *Why didn't he keep the letter? Maybe he didn't know it was in the book? He would most likely want it back if he knew.* That she was sure of. Sort of.

I should read the letter again to see if there are any clues, like his last name or contact information, then I could return the letter. Yes, that's what I'll do. She reread the letter—twice. Nothing. It was a letter he wrote to someone else and Katie had no right to read it. She refolded it and set it next to her.

Somehow, this letter made her think about her relationship with her ex-husband, Richard. He could have never anything like this. He was incapable of that kind of passion, that kind of tenderness. Richard could never be that open or vulnerable. There was raw emotion pouring from this man's heart. Jack's wife had been a very lucky woman. The letter gave her hope that there were still some good men out there.

Reluctantly, she pushed it further away from her. She still had two more large boxes to sort through and it was getting late. She pulled out the last book from the first box. It was a very large medical surgery book. Would any of her customers buy a medical book? She tossed it into her miscellaneous book pile.

The large book hit the pile with a thud, rolling over on its side. Something stuck out from the bottom of the book. A bookmark? Or another love note? She retrieved the book from the pile, opened it to the marked page and found a one hundred dollar bill.

Her mouth fell open in shock. What the heck is going on here? Didn't people check these things before they bring them to a flea market? She scrambled to her knees, now determined to go through every book she purchased from him. Katie was on a mission.

She searched through all the books from the first box, examining each one, turning them upside down and shaking them to see if anything came out before moving on to the next box of books. The second and third box yielded more money and other letters, each written on different colored paper.

When she opened the other ones she noticed each one had the same handwriting, signature, *Forever Jack* and the same opening, *My Dearest Darling*. All love letters written by Jack.

By the time she was finished, Katie had found in excess of three hundred dollars in cash and over thirty love letters. She could not believe all the money she had found but even so, the letters were more precious than money.

Katie sat there, with her found money in one hand and the love letters in the other. Taking the money, she put the bills into a plain white envelope and after sealing it, she wrote on the outside one word, *Jack*. She tucked it inside her cash register.

She sat down, made herself comfortable and took a deep breath. The second hand bookstore owner found she was unable to move, holding the treasured stack of correspondence close to her heart. She had read only one completely through but felt something happening inside of her, in her heart, something good.

Why didn't he just send his wife an email? A handwritten letter was much more romantic. But with an email it would get there faster, she debated with herself.

Katie arranged them by date, starting with the first one, dated February 2007. It was then she noticed that they all only included the month and year at the top of the page. Picking up another one she realized the letter she had read first was actually the second one he wrote.

Should she read them all now or ration them like her chocolates? Or should she just bundle them away? She was only going to read just one, but her curiosity got the better of her. She took another large sip of wine and settled in to read.

Maybe I can find out more about him, like his name and where he lives, and then I could return these letters to him, she reasoned.

Katie stopped for a moment but try as she might, she could not stop reading. After reading one she was compelled to reach for another. She felt urged on, she could not stop.

February, 2007

My Dearest Darling,

I miss you. Some feelings are expressed so simply. This separation is beyond my control, for you know if it was in my power I would be there, be there by your side. This journey will take time. Time that I know cannot be replaced. Like the sands of an hour glass, one grain at a time, it drops away, silently but evermore, never to be found again. I will write you. Be comforted by the fact you will always be in my thoughts...

Remember, just a short few weeks ago we celebrated New Year's Eve at the Grand Gala at the Club. You looked breathtaking in your shimmering evening gown and I know you loved me in my tux, as we danced around the dance floor. I love dancing with you. We both agreed those dance lessons certainly paid off, as we spiraled the Waltz together, moved to the beat of the Samba and Cha Cha and set the dance floor afire with the closeness of our Tango. The thunderous applause was always for you, your beauty and grace.

Then the band played your favorite song, 'MacArthur Park,' and you looked at me, grabbed my hand and the champagne, while we rushed to the beach to welcome in the New Year. Your gown was ruined from the choppy waves and my shoes were destroyed, but it was a New Year's Eve we will never forget. And while I hate the beach it was the best way to celebrate the New Year. We always believed that how you spend New Year's Eve is how you spend the rest of the year. Not this year, I am afraid, my love. I love you my dearest, always remember that. I must go.

Forever,

Jack

She studied the intimate correspondences, which spoke so eloquently to the love he obviously felt for his wife. Katie held it to her chest and took in a deep breath but so far she was no closer to finding out anything more about him. He had said he belonged to some club. What was the name of that club? She read the letter again. No luck.

Where was he writing from? Why was he writing? Why didn't he just go to her? Or call her? Was he in the Navy? In Africa? Why could he not call her or say anything about where he was? Maybe he was on a secret spy mission and could not tell her anything about it? But he was so handsome and seemed so honest. Maybe he was in jail? He didn't look like a jail bird though.

His letters sounded as if he could write volumes to this woman he loved. Katie refolded the letter on her lap. She read February and March and now fingered April in her hands. *No, these letters were too private and did not belong to her. They were not written to me. I am returning them tomorrow, she told herself. Yes, first thing tomorrow. I will call the people at the flea market and get his address from them and return them to him.* She smiled. It would be good to see him again.

April's letter was still in her hand, as she caressed it with her fingers. She was surrounded by piles of books on the floor and the precious letters on top of her as she lay on her sofa. Katie took another sip of wine, stroked the soft hair on Felix's back and thought about her wonderful day with the letter slipping from her hand. Her dreams swept her away into a land of love. A land she desperately wanted to visit. A place where she could fall in love again.

Chapter Two

Katie was awakened by a loud metallic tapping sound. *Tap, tap, tap.* She opened her eyes and found herself still lying on the sofa where she had fallen asleep the night before, right in front of the fireplace with the letters piled high on top of her. She had slept through the night, her first night without her horrible nightmare. The tapping began again. She looked at her watch—7:45 a.m.

She picked herself up and looked over the sofa. She heard the noise again. It was Donna McIntyre, always her first Monday morning customer. Donna wanted to be there bright and early so she could be first to peruse any new inventory. She was a very good customer.

Katie dragged herself from the sofa and unlocked the front door then opened it, causing the door chime to ring.

"Morning Kate, did you hear the news? They got him! They got the terrorist, *Numero Uno!* They sent in a SEAL team after locating him in Pakistan. Can you believe it? He was in Pakistan? Just where they thought he was all along. He was living in some big mansion. Go figure."

Kate moaned a sleepy reply to her loquacious customer.

"Got any good stuff? Any new books?" Donna finally asked, now getting down to the business at hand. The former school principal loved to thumb through books and would usually buy three to six, sometimes more.

Donna was tall and thin, looking like the old time stereotypical principal, just like the principal, Mrs. Moranski at Katie's grade school. She always wore a long black dress, even in the hot Florida sun. Her glasses were perched high on her forehead, and she wore a long silk scarf around her neck. She nearly shrieked when she saw the piles of books scattered on the floor around the sofa.

"Very good," Donna said to no one in particular. She grabbed a number of books and plopped down on the comfy sofa, lost to the world.

Katie looked through the large store front windows and noticed that for some reason the store seemed particularly dark and dreary even though the bright Florida sun shone bright. She tucked all of the letters into the side pocket of her wrinkled sweatshirt, examining the store and her longtime customer.

"Make yourself comfortable, Donna. I think I am going to take down these old drapes in the front, so it may get a little dusty in here. The place looks so dark."

"You know, you are right. I never noticed it before." Donna looked up from her growing stack of books on the floor next to the sofa.

A vision of bright light soon engulfed the shop.

"Wow, what a difference!" Donna said, when the huge green velour drapes came crashing down in a pile of dust.

Katie stood and admired her handiwork but then groaned when it became apparent the sunlight exposed the smudged, dirty windows at the front of the store. "Time for a bucket of water, some rags and Windex," she said to herself, as Donna was again engrossed in her own little book world.

When Katie was done the store was bright and airy. The front of the store shone like never before. She'd need to put some new plants in the front windows. She stood back by the sofa and breathed a deep sigh.

Her gaze fell on the small pile of medical books from the flea market. She picked them up and placed them on a shelf near the front of the store. She was not going to buy them but at the last moment figured, what the heck? Her customers were always surprising her as to what they would and would not buy. On top of the shelf she prominently displayed the largest and thickest book, titled, *The Surgeon's Guide to Thoracic and Cardiovascular Surgery*.

"There you go, Jack," she said to the black and green covered book. "See, even if you are not here, I can still talk to you. You can be my Wilson," she said. The book became her inanimate friend and confidant, just like in the movie *Cast Away*, with Tom Hanks.

"I'm sorry, Katie, did you say something to me?"

"No, I was just talking out loud. I do that a lot. Donna, I'm going upstairs to take a shower and will be back down soon. If you find anything you like, you know the drill, just leave the money on the register."

"Sure. Take your time. I'll keep an eye on things for you here."

"Hey Donna, I have a question for you."

"Sure," she said, without even looking up from her new hoard of books. "Fire away."

"If you found a love letter in an old book, would you read it?"

"Of course! But I would not know it was a love letter until I started reading it, you see. And besides, maybe it would have the person's address inside. Then, I would know where to return it. But I would also be curious as hell. Why? Are there any love letters in here?" she asked expectantly, finally looking up from her books, in hope of hearing a positive answer.

"No. No, there weren't any."

The door chimes sounded again as the front door opened and they both looked up to see one of Katie's strangest customers, Sidney, walk through the door. He was a fixture in Delray, another one of the quirky things about the small town that always amused Katie.

But looking at him in her shop always gave Katie chills, he wore the same clothes every time she saw him, torn and tattered with an old baseball cap covering his balding head. He always came in, asked for certain books and then not finding them, would turn and leave. *Strange dude with a peculiar homeless smell indeed*, Katie mused to herself. Some customers she could just do without. Once, she was pretty certain he'd followed one of her customers down the street. Katie thought he was just coming into her store to see her. He was definitely a strange dude.

"Morning," he mumbled to both of them. "Get any Raymond Chandler books in, Miss Kate?" His voice was slurred, making it sound more like accusation than a question.

"No, Sidney. No Raymond Chandler books today. Sorry." If she ever found any at a flea market she would not buy them, fearing it would keep him coming back for more but he never got the hint and kept coming back anyway.

He glanced at her, his dark brooding eyes chilling the room. He looked at them both for much too long, not saying a word, before turning and leaving without so much as a goodbye.

Once gone, Donna shivered, before saying, "Now there goes a mass murderer. But that's just my opinion," she quickly added.

"Yes, but so far he's been harmless," said Katie, trying to calm her down.

"Yeah, they say they are all like that and you never know what they are really thinking until something clicks inside their head and then boom, they explode. By then it's too late. Do you keep a gun in here, Kate?"

"No, I don't. Hey listen, I'll be back in a little while. I am just going upstairs for a bit. If you leave before I get back down just leave me a note with how many books you left with, okay?"

"Sure, Katie. No problem."

Katie clutched all of the letters and headed upstairs. She sat down with a sigh on her bed, laying the letters down beside her, anxious to read more. Felix came from his secret space underneath the bed and slid next to her, purring, rubbing against her.

Reading the letters was becoming addictive but she needed to know what was said even though it was a one way conversation. Maybe she could just read one more while the water heated for her shower.

April, 2007

My Dearest Darling,

I have tried to...

The phone rang and a startled Katie jumped to attention. "Hello," she said, almost under her breath, feeling as if she had been caught red-handed reading someone else's diary.

"Katie. Katie is that you? It's Jess. Hello?"

"Hi, Jess. I wasn't sure who was calling. My caller ID isn't working."

"Oh. Are we still on for lunch today?"

"Yeah, sure, I'll close the shop for an hour around noon. Meet you at Tony's?" It was a local pizza hangout just minutes from the store.

"Great. What are you doing today?" Jess asked.

"Well, I was going to try to do some things around here, you know? File the books I just bought and I want to spruce the place up... and maybe do some... painting."

"Painting?" Jessie asked anxiously.

"Yeah, painting."

"What kind of painting?" she asked.

"The front door needs a new paint job. The landlord will take forever to do it so I figured I have some left over paint, so I thought I would go ahead do the entrance."

"Oh, okay Kate, I was just curious. I thought maybe you might be painting something artistic. Hey, we also said we would try to do dinner tonight, right? What do you think about dinner at City Oyster, outside table?"

"That sounds good."

"Hey, maybe we can even have Ollie wait on us? You know, I think he is kind of sweet on you."

"Oh, give me a break. I am old enough to be his… older sister." Katie did not really know what to say, being so engrossed in the letters. She hung up with Jess and looked at the letter lying next to her again. She was at first tempted to pick it up and read it. But she knew what she had to do first. Kate picked up her cell phone, checked her contacts and speed dialed the number.

"Hi, this is Katie Kosgrove," she said when they finally answered the phone after seven rings. "I was at the Atlantic Avenue Flea Market yesterday and I bought some things. When I got home I found something of value inside. I would like to return it to its rightful owner."

"Is that so, dear?" said the overly disinterested woman on the other end of the line.

"Yes, it is. All I know is his first name was Jack and he had the stall next to the watchmaker, Time something or other was the name on the stall next to his booth. The man I am looking for I believe he was a first timer. I had never seen him at the market before."

"Yes, dear?" she continued. "How do you think I can help you?"

"Well I thought if you could give me his contact information then I could return this item to him."

"I'm sorry dearee, that's against our policy. We cannot hand out anyone's address or phone number. Sorry I couldn't be of more help," she said, ready to hang up.

"But you don't understand. I found some love letters in some books I bought from him and I think he would want them back. Please, can't you help me?"

"Love letters? What kind of love letters?" The woman, for the first time, seemed fully awake and very interested in what Katie had to say.

"You know, love letters written by a loving husband to his wife. That kind of love letter."

"Well dear, if you brought them by here and left them with me, I will make sure that he gets them back."

"Can't you just look up his information for me? Please?"

"Well… okay. Wait a minute. That was this past weekend, right?"

"Yes, yesterday's monthly flea market."

"You said he had the stall next to About Time, the watch repair guy?"

"Yes, that's it! That's the one!" Katie said, nearly shouting at the woman.

"That would be stall #349. Well, he was a late registrant. Did you read the letter dear? Maybe the letter or envelope would have his address inside."

"I checked already, there was no envelope and no address."

"Oh," moaned the disappointed woman. "Yes, here it is. Stall #349, he registered the day of the flea market and paid cash upon arrival. I have no information at all on your letter writing friend. I'm sorry, dear."

"Does it at least show a name on your roster? A city? Perhaps a phone number? A last name? Anything?"

"No dear. It just shows he paid cash on Sunday, that's all. Sorry I could not be more helpful."

"Thanks anyway," she said.

On a hunch Katie checked the Delray Beach phone directory and found the phone number for the people who had the stall next to Jack that day, About Time. A tired voice, sounding far away answered the phone.

"Hello, it's about time," came the sad sounding answer. "Can I help you?"

"Yes , I hope so. This is Katie Kosgrove, I was at the flea market on Atlantic and stopped by the booth next to yours. I bought something from a man named Jack there and when I go home I found something I am sure he would like back. Were you there?"

"Yep. I'm the only one here. I remember him, Jack or Jake or John something like that."

"Yes, that's him," Katie said, now getting excited by the mere mention of Jack's name.

"Nice guy," came the calm voice on the phone. "Tall dark and handsome type right?"

"Yes, that's the one. Ah… but I didn't notice if he was tall or handsome," Katie said, trying not to sound like a stalker.

"Well, a lot of the other ladies that came by sure did, got to tell you. But I don't think he has ever been to a flea market before. He was really disorganized, but a really nice guy. He helped me load my truck back up when it started to rain. How can I help you?"

"I need to find him to return these things to him. Do you know his last name or where he lives?"

"Nope, we didn't talk about things like that, just about watches, timepieces and the like," said the tired voice. "As a matter of fact, he even bought an old Elgin watch from me. It was a nice watch, but I don't think he needed a watch, since he was already wearing one. I think he was just trying to help me out. Sorry I can't help you."

Katie started to hang up the phone when she heard him perk up and say, "Wait, wait just a minute. I had him fill out a warranty card for me. You know I don't sell junk. I warranty all of my watches for a full thirty days. Yes indeed, thirty days. You won't find any other watchmaker selling used watches give you that kind of warranty. Hold on let me check my warranty cards. Can you hold for a minute?"

"Yes, yes of course, I can hold," Katie said enthusiastically her hopes rising.

He was back a few moments later, "I got it right here. Let me put my glasses on, just be a sec. Yep here it is, 10k gold Elgin watch, square face, brown lizard band. He wrote in the contact info only, John P. and under address, he wrote the word, local. Nothing else, sorry ma'am."

"Thanks," Katie said hanging up the phone. A dead end.

Disappointed she grabbed her hat, threw on an old pair of jeans, t-shirt and headed back downstairs. Donna was already gone but left fifteen dollars lying on the cash register and a note with the list of books she bought.

The front door took more time to paint than she thought but the rhythmic movement of the brush entranced her and she went with the flow. She wished now after finishing the door that she had more things to paint.

She walked inside the store and her gaze alighted on the blank canvases Jess gave her a few days ago—begging her to begin painting once more—now positioned on the easel. She saw Donnas' handiwork in moving things around the store, her organizational efforts to rearrange items to be able to peruse her new trove of books. Katie rubbed her nose with her green paint-stained hand and walked towards the blank canvas.

"Your life is a blank canvas," her mother always told her. "It *is* what you make of it." Her mother was wonderful and taught Kate a lot, but she also remembered her mother's advice, "Never marry a man who won't listen to you or who doesn't respect you, no matter how sexy he may appear." Unfortunately, neither of them had taken that advice to heart. She remembered, when she married Richard the things she championed in her life were slowly snuffed out.

Oh, how she had missed painting. Missed the art galleries she'd owned. She had always loved to paint, she also cherished the time she spent reading, jogging, but one by one her passions withered away. She didn't know why she didn't start painting earlier after she divorced Richard, maybe she was afraid the passion had died. The passions in her life had become distant memories.

"How can I do this?" Katie rubbed her nose again and retrieved the brush and the artist's knife from the box. She grabbed the palette board and squeezed large amounts of paint onto it, the distinctive odor of fresh oil paint filled the air.

She closed her eyes, took a deep breath and for a brief moment, did nothing but let her mind drift. She thought of the letters. A vision came to mind. When she reopened her eyes, she saw things more clearly. The paintbrush came alive in her hand. She began to mix her paint, matching the colors.

She wielded the brush like a delicate instrument, with artistry and craft. She stroked the artist's knife, laying paint on the canvas in deep, dark colors, swirling left, then right, blues, reds, yellows appeared on the canvas, magically blending together.

The driven artist added more colors and worked with fervor until she was finished. She worked like one possessed, the way she painted many years before. Why did she ever give it up?

"Like that," she said out loud, stepping back, refreshed. The colors were so vivid, the drawing so insightful, she thought to herself, as her creation jumped off the drying canvas. Having worked on it no longer than the time a butterfly spends on a flower, she had created something beautiful. Something wonderful and magical.

Chapter Three

After feeding Felix, Katie grabbed her second cup of coffee, and pulled her sandy colored hair back behind her head, pinning it tight with a tortoise shell pin. She grabbed an old pair of sweatpants, which had been cut off and converted to baggy grey shorts. She then threw on a yellow, oversized Key West t-shirt, her best camouflage to hide the accumulated weight she had picked up over the ten months since her divorce. Her hands still contained the many telltale signs of her morning painting adventures.

It was a cool early May morning, having rained steadily the night before, dropping the temperature by some ten degrees. It was a constant rain, as it was most nights this time of year, chilling the night air. Katie enjoyed the welcome relief that the showers brought. She slept well last night, no nightmare kept her awake.

Her devouring dream kept her up most nights, the same dream every night. She was chasing the same elusive person up some stairs but never caught him. Her psychiatrist told her it was her way of wanting to try to recapture the past days of her married life. Katie fired her shrink, which made her feel better but it did not help stop the nightmares.

Last night when she finally drifted off into restful sleep, she could hear the faint but distinct sound of a whistle, sweet, melodic, not loud, just pure. She mimicked the sound on her lips, the melody floated in her mind.

"Time to go," she told Felix, half expecting an answer from the intelligent black and white misfit. "I can't be late for Jessie again," she said. Felix could have cared less about Jessie except that she would bring him treats when she visited; he was only interested in milk and something to eat. Slipping on her trusty sandals, she skipped down the outside steps to the front of the store after saying good bye to Felix.

Jessie used to work as a gallery manager for Katie in New York at one of the art galleries. That was before Jessie came to Florida to open her antique store on trendy Atlantic Avenue. Jess called Katie after her divorce and invited her to come to live in Florida.

"You'll love it," she remembered Jessie saying. "The weather is great, the people are friendly and it is so laid back." Jessie had become a good friend during Katie's trying times after her divorce and she was always there for her when she needed someone to talk to in the middle of the night.

As Katie walked past the glass front door of her bookshop, out of habit, she tugged on the door handle to make sure it was locked and checked to make sure her "Out to Lunch" sign was visible from the street.

She caught a glimpse of her reflection in the storefront glass as she passed by. She forgot to put on her makeup and lipstick and touched her chest to make sure she had put on a bra. *One out of three ain't bad.* A natural beauty is what they used to call her at the modeling agency when she was in college, yeah but, if they could only see her now.

Katie looked at the old masonry building where she worked and lived. It was off a side street just past the trendy Pineapple Grove District of Downtown Delray Beach. The old former general store was surrounded by dense palm trees and by overgrown mahogany trees, which kept out the sweltering hot afternoon sun.

The building overlooked a nearby canal and from her second floor apartment, if she stood on her tiptoes, she could catch a glimpse of the ocean, some eight blocks away. The rear of the building provided complete privacy because of the canal and overgrown brush. She did not even need curtains since no one lived behind her—not that they'd be able to see anything with the brush. She used only a drape to cover the windows during the cool winter nights to keep out the wind.

"Ugh!" Her bike tire was flat. She'd have to walk the eight blocks to Tony's. She did not have a car, since she no longer had a valid driver's license, but she knew she could always count on Jessie to drive if she needed a ride. She probably ought to renew her license at some point, but she'd just never got around to it when it expired years earlier. "I'll get one," she would always say, "soon," but she never did. She used her bike to get around Delray and was perfectly happy to be able to do that. "I can walk or bike to anyplace I need to go," she told everyone.

She smiled to herself, as she walked, reminiscing the first time she saw Jack a few days ago at his flea market stall. He was a tall handsome man with a few wisps of graying hairs mixed in with his dark brown hair wildly protruding from the side under his dark sunglasses.

Walking closer to see what he was selling, she'd glanced at him. By the looks of his wares, he was a "downsizer" with a wide range of eclectic items stacked high on the tables and with boxes lined up high behind him.

The bookstore veteran could tell he was a first timer, just by his inefficient organization and lack of prices on everything he had on display. He removed his sunglasses and tucked them in the front pocket of his old chambray work shirt, still busy trying to figure out what he should do next. *Definitely a first timer,* thought Katie.

He turned around to put more items on the large table and their eyes met. He had piercing dusty blue eyes, a gentle smile with a rugged manly look about him that she liked. He was handsome enough he could have played in the old cowboys movies she loved to watch on late night television but he also had a certain sadness about him. Nothing she could put her finger on but it was there nonetheless. His khaki shorts and his white sneakers looked new, with hardly a scuff mark on the front of the shoes. He looked to be somewhat older than her, say fiftyish, but very good-looking.

She would never forget the first time their eyes met and he smiled at her. Now she did not know how to get in touch with him. She thought about everything he said for a clue. What was the name of the area he moved from, Delray Shore, Bear Club. She could not remember. Maybe Jess could come up with something. Or maybe she would run into him again at next week's flea market.

She soon found herself at Tony's and grabbed a window table just inside for her and Jessie. The lunchtime crowd was just starting to stream into this popular local hangout. But Katie did not notice much because increasingly all she could think of was – Jack.

Chapter Four

"What were you daydreaming about?" asked Jessie, handing her a fresh cup of coffee she picked up from the counter.

"Hi Jess. I was thinking about nothing in particular, just daydreaming'."

Her friend sat down across from her and smiled when she looked at Kate. Taking a deep breath Jess said, "You need to go joggin' with me again. Get back into shape. We used to have a great time. And you need a car. No self-respecting woman your age rides a bike anymore."

"Yeah, yeah, Jess. Exercise will kill me now since I am so out of shape. And I never needed a car in New York and I don't need one here. Everything is so close."

"Well, this ain't New York Toto and another thing, you need to move your shop closer to Atlantic Avenue where the action and the customers are, that's what you need. And you need to get back into painting, artistic painting. God, you were such a great painter. I loved your work."

"But I did do a small painting this morning." Katie grinned.

"Really? Fantastic! That is great news. Keep on painting. What did you do?"

"I did an abstract sunrise."

Katie graduated from Brown University with a degree in English Literature and Fine Arts. She'd taken many art appreciation classes and discovered she was an exceptionally talented painter. She surprised herself since she had always been a tomboy growing up.

She worked in New York as an art editor but still painted at night and sold her artwork to local galleries. Katie ultimately took the leap and opened her own gallery in mid-town Manhattan. It was so successful she opened two other galleries across the city. Then she met Richard, a very successful New York real estate attorney and after a whirlwind courtship they were married. In a few years he'd convinced her she did not need to work any longer, so one by one, she closed down her galleries. She regretted her decision every day since she gave it all up.

Their food came and the server, a young girl with three lip rings sporting blonde and purple hair, set the steaming cheese pizza down between them and left.

"Could we get some plates, napkins and eating utensils, please?" Jessie asked the young girl while she walked away.

"Yeah sure, whatever," she said without even turning around.

"How are you going to track him down?" Jess asked.

"Who?"

"Who? Are you daft? You know damn well who I mean. Your new friend Jack. And don't think you can fool me, I saw that look."

"I have *no* idea what you mean."

"Okay, okay have it your way. But I'm telling you right now, you'll never catch a man like that one unless you tackle him and wrestle him to the ground."

"Seems to work well for you Jessie, huh?" Katie retorted.

"Ha, ha, funny, girlfriend. But seriously, any luck tracking him down?"

"No, no luck at all. I thought maybe something he said to you may be of help. Do you remember anything?"

"Other than he was tall, dark and incredibly sexy and handsome, I don't remember a thing. But at least you got a pile of books from him. Maybe there was a name inside one of them. Check it out."

"Good idea, but I have already done that." An art gallery van passed them on its way to making a delivery, a fairly common sight in Delray.

"Kate, remember how much you used to get for just one of your paintings when we were in New York at the art gallery? Now how many books do you have to sell to make any money at all?"

Katie was glad for the change in subject. "Jess, I do this because I love doing it. I don't do it for the money. I love books and doing what you love is the most important thing, you know? Right?"

"Yeah sure, Sir Lancelot," glummed Jessie.

Jessie looked at her good friend and a smile broke out on her face. Katie had always been there for her anytime Jess needed her and she was such a sweetheart. She deserved better than someone like Richard. They paid the bill and Jessie offered to drop her back at the bookstore.

"Did Richard stop paying his alimony again? I'm telling you, you don't need that jerk."

"No, he keeps paying like clockwork but I don't want his money and don't need it. I have plenty in the bank from the sale of the galleries to do whatever I want. I don't want to ever rely on him or any other man ever again, so I put his checks right into the bank and just let the money sit there earning interest. Don't start Jess, come on. It's too early and I didn't sleep well last night."

"Ah, still trying to get used to sleeping alone are you? Well Katie, you keep wearing clothes like that and I can guarantee that you will be sleeping alone for a really long time," she said, backing the van out onto Third Avenue, blasting her horn at a sedan which had the temerity to cut her off.

"Old fart," Jessie proclaimed under her breath. She pointed the van towards downtown Delray and they were on their way.

"What's wrong with my clothes?" Katie asked, yanking on her favorite t-shirt.

"If you have to ask me, then you're in worse shape than I thought and I know you have not been out on a date since the divorce. Right? Am I right?" Jessie asked, running a second red light.

"No, I have not but that is a conscious decision on my part," Katie replied, nervously sipping her coffee.

"How *is* Richard and his young trollop by the way?" Jess asked dryly.

"I don't know we haven't talked."

They pulled up to a stoplight and Jessie turned toward her. "Baby, listen to me, he ain't coming back to you and besides you know my opinion of him and the whole situation. I think you are better off without him. You spent sixteen years with the dude and where did it get you? You have to snap out of your funk and get on with livin' girl. Do you hear me?"

Katie's response was muffled by the sound of a horn honking at them, impolitely urging them to move on.

"Keep your pants on bud," Jessie bellowed outside the van window. "I'll move when I'm good and ready to move." She stepped on the gas, causing the van to jerk forward and throw Katie back in her seat.

"I'm glad we don't have any mirrors or breakables in the back," Katie joked, causing them to both break out laughing. Jessie owned a small antique store just off Second Avenue in downtown Delray and sold anything you could imagine for a beach house. She had a very loyal following and her van was usually filled with old lamps, mirrors, sea shells and the like.

"What is that tune you've been humming?"

"I don't know. All of sudden this morning it just like popped into my mind and I can't get rid of it."

"It's catchy."

"So, back to Jack… Why didn't you give him your phone number? Or better yet get his number?"

"I wasn't thinking, that's all."

"The guy kept looking you in the eye," she said, "They say if a man looks you in the eye for more than six seconds straight, he either wants to murder you or have sex. And kiddo, I don't think that good looking hunk of a man was any murderer. What am I going to do with you, Kate?" Jess turned onto the main road and sped towards home.

"Dinner tonight? Seven? City Oyster?"

"Yeah. Sounds great."

"This will be a record."

"What?"

"Getting together with you three times in two days. See ya later, I gotta go." She pulled out of the gravel parking lot in front of the used bookstore, her tires squealing when they came in contact with the old asphalt side road.

Chapter Five

Katie unlocked the door to her shop and flipped around the sign announcing she was now "OPEN" for business. She tilted her head, studying the canvas she painted in the morning. Walking toward her most recent work of art, she felt good looking at it. She still had her talent, it hadn't died with her marriage.

She sank into the old sofa, soon joined by Felix and retrieved one of Jack's letters from her pocket.

July, 2007

My Dearest Darling,

I awoke this morning to the scent of freshly cut grass hanging in the air and it reminded me of our picnics high on the hill overlooking the river. Remember?

On our way there, you always insisted on stopping by the small nearby cemetery and paying respects to the unknown dearly departed. You stopped to pull weeds from around the neglected headstones. You always said it was the least we could do, since no one else seemed to care.

I always loved that about you, the way you cared so much for strangers, little children and those who needed a champion. You were so kind to everyone. I miss that in this world of "me first" or "me only" attitudes. I was always so touched by your sincere caring for those you never knew.

Afterwards we spread our blanket under the shadow of the tall oak tree, which overlooked the river and we watched the barges travel by with their long loads, mesmerizing our senses with their rhythmic approach to life.

I recall your hand picked blades of grass from my shirt and gently moved the hair from my forehead. I remember your kiss as we lay on the blanket, the world now filled with only two people, you and me. I miss those wondrous days. Miss you. I must go now.

Forever,

Jack

Invigorated by his letter, she reached for the second, larger canvas. Taking a deep breath, she closed her eyes and thought about sunrises and sunsets. Katie thought of the beach, the river. Then she thought of the letters. She reopened her eyes and began to paint.

She added more colors to her ever growing palette board and let her soul *and* her passion direct her brush. She was in heaven, taking her time to enjoy it, like she would a fine wine or an evening of wondrous lovemaking.

Painting, she now remembered the wonders of light and the treachery of darks. She held her brush stiff for the lines and soft for curves, then she backed away, only to return to paint yet again. She worked with renewed spirit. But this was not work, this was pure joy. Her pure passion.

Slow at first, as if stepping into an unknown pool of water, she painted until she found her sea legs, while the slashes of brilliant colors and unknown shapes suddenly came alive on the canvas. The sun contained amber glory and the sea was foaming and wild as she continued to deliver stroke after stroke, all in vibrant color. She used her re-awakened fingers to add paint on the canvas, giving depth and texture from one side to the other. She worked passionately without regard to time and place.

She moved almost trancelike, with the fever of one possessed. Her painting said it in a convincing and contradicting fashion, the sea was calm, the sea was churning, the sun shone bright, the sun was violent. Her creation was spellbinding. It was not a race but a test of endurance to see who would win: her, the paint, the colors, or the sea. Finally she was done, nearly exhausted. She stepped away from the tumultuous canvas as it started to dry in the afternoon heat.

The finished product looked different depending on the view of the canvas. The paint was thick, curled and deep. The colors seen on one side were hardly noticeable from the opposite direction. The reds, vibrant in one view, were dull from the other and the blues deep and shiny from the left were calming from the right.

"Yes," she said quietly. "Yes." She could have painted for hours more, but she did not want to be late for her dinner with Jess. The time went by so quickly but she looked at it and was pleased. She was finished. *Have to go*, she thought, turning once more to admire her creation.

Katie showered, scrubbing off the old green door paint, along with the new speckled colors which peppered her hands. She wrapped the canvas and then lugged her freshest creation down Second Ave, past the plaza towards the evening's action. In a few short blocks, she was on the bustling street affectionately known as "The Avenue" or more commonly called Atlantic Avenue.

The revitalization of Delray Beach began fifteen years earlier. The city fathers granted a property tax moratorium for any business willing to come downtown and invest in the area to help create jobs. The street became the new Miami Beach without the crime. Cafes, diners and fine restaurants, art galleries, micro-brew pubs quickly lined the street with a total of nearly sixty dining options competing for business. Their plan worked and business was very good.

Part-time residents, who had restaurants in New York, quickly opened a second location on Atlantic Avenue. It was, as they said, a no-brainer. The food and ambiance was unparalleled and you could safely walk anywhere on the people-filled street at night, without fear of crime. It was a great place to live and Katie loved it.

She walked past the deserted Varnberg's furniture store, the last of the old time hold outs on Atlantic, now gone. She peeked inside the cavernous store. The now empty location had a large expanse of open space and many large windows facing the ocean. A *For Lease / For Sale* sign was posted in the middle of the front window.

Her painting had made her feel alive, as though she were her old self again. This deserted old building would make for a perfect art gallery. It had lots of foot and vehicular traffic and high visibility to boot. Was she ready for it? *This could be very interesting.* She glanced at her watch. She was going to be late and rushed off to meet her best friend.

Jess had secured an outside, sidewalk table by the corner. Katie waved at her but could tell from the look on her face that she was upset. Jessie hated it when anyone was late, but her face seemed to lighten when she saw what Katie was carrying.

"Hiya." Katie set down her load without making any reference to it. "Did you order wine for me?"

"Chardonnay? Yes, of course I did," responded Jessie, glancing at the large wrapped picture canvas behind them, with the ends poking out obtrusively from under the brown paper.

Katie picked up a menu and began perusing the daily specials, purposefully ignoring the canvas near them. She was enjoying the way Jess appeared to be fighting the urge to ask what it was. "Do you know where the oysters are from that they are serving tonight?" asked Katie nonchalantly.

"Prince Edward Islands, Canada," Jessie replied. "Okay, okay. You made your point. What is it?"

"This is the reason I was late." Katie jumped up and set the painting on a nearby empty seat. She tore a corner off the paper covering, but stopped. "It's for you, Jess. Tell me what you think. Be honest, okay? But if you hate it, don't say so, all right?"

"All right already," Jessie agreed, and Katie let the last of the stiff brown, wrapping paper fall to the sidewalk.

"Oh. My. God." Jessie put her hands to her face, covering her mouth. "Kate it is your best work ever. Oh my god, I love it!"

"Okay, okay. Now you can tell me the truth. Do you like it? Is it any good?"

"Katie, I mean it. It is great! I absolutely love it."

"Really?" Katie beamed. "You really like it? Really?" Passersby and other patrons seated at the other outside tables nearby came by to admire the painting. Murmurs of appreciation and compliments filled the air.

"Yes," said Jess. "I really like it. This is fantastic! It's as if you never stopped painting. It looks so inspired."

Katie's face froze. "But do you think it will sell? You know times have changed, people's tastes have changed. I can only paint what I feel. I don't do it for anyone else, I paint for me. My paintings reflect how I feel not really the feelings of others."

Jessie studied the painting closely and observed, "Then you must be feeling pretty good, Kate. This is great work. I mean it."

"Well, I just don't know about…"

Jessie jumped up, grabbing the painting. "Order me another Merlot and I'll be right back."

Katie tried to stop her. "Wait! Where are you going? Come on Jess, let's have some dinner." But it was no use. Jess was gone in a flash.

Katie finished her first wine and ordered another when their young, twenty-something waiter asked her again if she was ready to order. The intrusive young waiter motion towards the growing line of impatient diners, waiting for the preferred outside table on the sidewalk. Katie offered up what she hoped was an apologetic look and craned her neck to see if Jess was on her way back.

Her usual, overly friendly waiter Ollie stopped by to say hello. "Katie, it's so good to see. How have you been?"

"I'm good. I started painting again and my life is looking up. Sorry you are not our waiter tonight. Maybe next time we come."

"Absolutely. I saw the painting you did, it was fantastic. Sorry, I have customers waiting, I gotta go. See ya Kate." He gave her a long admiring glance before walking away. "Keep it up."

It was then she saw Jessie walking towards her with a huge smile on her face and still carrying the painting under her arm.

"Where did you go?"

"Down the street to Pollack's Art Gallery," she said, barely able to restrain her enthusiasm.

"I asked him what he thought and he told me he loved it and wanted to display it in his gallery or take it on consignment. And do you know how much he thought he could get for it?"

"No," responded Katie. "I have been out of the art world for a while. How much did he think they could get for it?"

Jess took the napkin from under her now very warm Merlot and borrowing a pen from the young snip of a waiter, wrote down a number.

"Whoa! You're kidding, right?" The number was three times higher than she had ever sold any of her other paintings for in the past.

"No, Katie, I'm not kidding. He loved it. He said he could sell as many as I could deliver."

"Sell it if you like, Jess. My feelings won't be hurt. That's a lot of money."

"No, never! Are you kidding me? Katie I would not *dare* sell it. I told you, I love it. But you know your passion is painting and you know you are very good at the work you do. Look closely at this piece you painted. But it's up to you now."

Jess looked at her close friend and let the message she was saying, and not saying, sink in. "Come on let's eat, I'm starved."

They sat with the painting sitting upright in the empty chair between them, as their silent guest of honor and ordered dinner. Katie was lost deep in thought.

"Katie, this painting is really very good. It is the best I have ever seen you do. What's behind all of this?"

She thought about it for a moment before answering. "Let me ask you something. If you found a love letter in an old book, would you read it?"

"Of course I would! Is the Pope Catholic? Why? Did you find one?"

Katie paused for a minute before looking up from her salad. "You remember the man I bought the boxes of books from at the flea market?"

"You mean Mr. Marlborough Man? The dreamy delicious guy? Of course I remember him. Why?"

"Well, I found a letter he wrote to his wife which was left in one of the books I bought from him."

"Yeah? And? Did you read it? Do you have it with you? I know you still haven't had any luck locating him. Maybe we can get an address off of the letter and call him, you know? We can return it to him. I am sure he would want it back." Jess sounded excited at the prospects.

"There was no name, other than Jack, no address listed, and no envelope."

"Well, we already know his name was Jack. Did you call the people who run the Atlantic Market?"

"I called them. They told me he registered late and paid cash. They have no record of his name or any other information about him." They continued their brainstorming in between bites of food.

"I even called the guy who had the booth next to him. No luck there either. All he knew is that Jack lives locally."

"Well, that's a start at least. Hmm. Did you check the other books? Maybe there were more letters."

"I checked. No luck." She decided, for some unknown reason, not to share the information about the other ones she had found. "Reading the letter felt odd, like it was a betrayal. It was like he wrote it to someone else and I was eavesdropping. But Jess from his letters, it was obvious that he loved her so very much."

"Katie, now you really have me going. I don't know what to tell you. But I have to say, from the looks of him, he is certainly worth looking into, you know what I mean?" Jessie's cell phone rang and the way her friend's eyes lit up, Katie knew immediately it was Jessie's current love interest Mickey on the other end.

Mickey was an over the road trucker and would call when he was on his way into town. Katie was not crazy about him but Jessie really loved the guy. Katie often wondered how many Jessies he had scattered across the country. But one thing was for sure, he made Jess happy and that is all that mattered. Katie just didn't want her to get hurt.

"Got to go Katie, my girl. He's one hour North on I-95 and on his way here to Delray. God, have I missed him. You want a lift home?"

"No, you go ahead. Since it is such a beautiful evening, I think I'll just walk home. Tell Mickey I said hello." With a kiss on Katie's cheek and a smile on her lips Jess was gone, on her way to meet the love of her life.

Katie walked home from the restaurant and was so preoccupied with all of the thoughts swirling around in her head that she did not notice the jogger following her on the other side of the street. She crossed the road and he moved nearer to her. Soon she was home, showered and ready to plop into bed. Dark eyes from underneath the huge Mahogany trees watched her. Watched her undress through the large rear windows, waiting. Waiting and watching.

Chapter Six

Katie was very busy over the next couple of weeks painting and scouring the streets of Delray Beach for information. She wanted to gather information from other store owners on how business was going. Were they busy? Was it a good time to open another storefront? Did they think it was going to get better or worse? They were all forthcoming with encouragement and good ideas. These were business people that were right on the avenue and if anyone had a sense of the day to day economy for art, and high end sculptures, they would surely be the ones. She was sheltered from it all at her location and the nature of what she sold.

She got lots of help but every time she ran into a roadblock or if she had a problem, she would ask the surgeon's guidebook, her Wilson so to speak, so proudly displayed on the top shelf of her new, "Medical Book Section." The new section consisted of five medical books she found in the boxes she bought from Jack. They did not sell but that was fine since they reminded her of him.

She addressed the book softly, other times, inquisitively. "Jack, am I crazy for thinking about doing this again? Should I wait?" Each time he gave her the answer she needed with an all knowing silence.

Katie jogged nearly every day now, making her way around town. Her first day out she nearly collapsed from the running but it did get easier each day as she went down all of the Delray side streets. Soon she was jogging back and forth to the ocean. Her life was becoming fulfilled again. Now she felt she had purpose. Her muscles toned the more she ran and her thoughts became clearer.

She was in and out of every store on Atlantic Avenue, asking questions of the employees, meeting with store and restaurant owners. She walked past the old furniture store, Varnbergs, lingering longer each time. Needing a break, she sat at an outside table in front of coffee shop and gazed longingly at her purse. The letters were in there. She could wait no more. She wrenched open her bag like a woman starved and unfolded another of her treasures.

December, 2007

My Dearest Darling,

I have tried to recite the poems you loved so much and had even thought of trying to write some myself. But I cannot hold a candle to your eloquence. Remember, 'I will take my life into my hands, and I will use it?' Remember those words? Sing those words. Sing loud and sing clear, they are almost as understanding as your poetry.

Are you writing? Write of us. Write of times we shared and spent together, my love. Write of the things we discovered and loved. Remember walking the beach in 'Raytown,' your pet name for Delray? Remember Café Luna, table six, by the window?

Remember the large butter-like pads of baked garlic, floating in olive oil. We would spread it like butter on fresh Italian bread. So sweet, but I still don't know what their recipe was to make it so fine and wonderful. Remember the pillow-like softness of the gnocchi? The sweet homemade rosemary and basil pesto? The delicious Chianti you love? And the Sangiovese for me. The best!

And then we would go dancing at the JW Beach Hotel nearby on the beach. Remember reading poems in bed to each other, until we fell fast asleep. Lying so close to you, I could smell the sweetness of your perfume. I loved touching your hair. I can still feel the softness in my hands.

What do I remember most of all? I recall the simple touch, the smile from across the room that you would send to my heart and make me feel as if I was the only one in the crowded room. I was always the touchy feely kind of guy and it pierces my heart to be denied the treasure of your touch. I do miss you so. One takes so many things for granted until they are denied and the desire is heightened. I remember—

Oh, thou hallowed heart rings true,
Thy deep abode in dark so fires my soul
Thru the darkest hours I have yearned of thee,
Must I be gone, to have my heart ring so loud,
Whilst you return to me
Thy arms, eyes, smile and thee

See, I remember my love. Write poetry in your heart, hold it close, save it and we shall cuddle before the fireplace and read 'til dawn. I must go now. Soon, my love, soon.

I love you, my dearest.

Forever,

Jack

Katie was always touched by the raw emotions in the man's letters. She knew of some of the places he wrote about. Somehow, she wished she could have been there with him, she wished those letters would have been written to her but she knew it was not meant to be. She felt as if he had been talking to her, urging her on to greater accomplishments. But she knew better, she knew they were written to his one and only Dearest Darling and she was only a bystander reading his words. Still, his words gave her strength. She closed her eyes and remembered.

She fingered his next letter, treating it with increased respect. As she read each correspondence, one by one she was touched by his love and understanding. She was consumed with her quest for knowing and understanding more about this man, he who wrote letters so trustful, so truthful and so powerful.

A couple of months went by without her seeing Jess. Katie had even gone to the Atlantic Market by herself because Jessie had rushed to Chicago when her aunt became ill. She thoroughly searched the flea market but there was no mysterious Jack in attendance.

Thankfully, Jess was back from Chicago, and Katie picked up the phone to call her.

"Hey Jess, how's your Aunt?"

"Better, I guess. Back to normal and complaining again. So I guess that is good," said Jessie, with worry still obvious in her voice.

"You want to do lunch and maybe some shopping?"

"Shopping? Sure Kate. What kind?"

"Ah… some clothes shopping."

Jessie, always the clothes aficionado, never passed up an opportunity to go clothes or shoe shopping. Or shop for any clothes for that matter but it was a rarity for Katie to even step into a clothing store.

"Clothes shopping? Sure! But you haven't bought any clothes in ages. What's going on?"

"Well, I am turning over a new leaf. One that I think you would be proud of."

"Okay then, if you are serious, let me help you my dear. I know you can't do this alone. I tell you what, I will make the extreme sacrifice and we can make it an entire day of clothing shopping if you like. I'll pick you up at two o'clock. Okay?"

"Sure. Got to go." Steam from the shower billowed from her bathroom door, looking more like a lingering, low level fog.

• • • • •

Jessie was locking up her house was and turned with wide, surprised eyes when Katie's new, big, silver SUV pulled into her parking lot. She honked for extra affect.

"Get a move on girlfriend, if you want to find the deals!" shouted Katie.

"What? You can't drive without a license?"

"Lots to talk about Jess, hop in," she said, with a satisfied grin on her face. They headed towards downtown Delray. Katie stopped at the light on Atlantic and as they sat there, patiently waiting for the light to turn green, she pointed to the old furniture store. "Sad about Varnbergs pulling out, isn't it?"

"Yeah, but that big old space will get snapped up quickly. It's in a prime location." Jess turned to look at the old furniture store. "See I told you, they are already fixing it up for a new tenant."

"Yes?" responded Katie, in mock surprise.

"Yeah," said Jess. "It says, *Coming Soon, a new art gallery, Katherine's.*"

"Is that so?" Katie queried.

Jessie turned to look at her friend, when she realized the connection. "What is this?"

"I told you I turned over a new leaf, one you would be proud of, remember? I bought the building a couple weeks back. The downstairs will be my gallery and the upstairs I am setting up as an art school to help train and develop the next generation of artists and my apartment too."

"What about the bookstore?"

"Do you remember Donna, the principal? Well, it turns out she always wanted to own a bookstore. So on a trial basis she is going to run it for awhile and see how she likes it. It works all the way around."

Jessie beamed at her longtime friend. When they finally pulled into Natalia's, the chic downtown clothing store, Jess hugged Kate and kissed her on the cheek.

"I am so proud of you. I can't tell you how proud of you I am." She tugged at her shirt and felt her waist. "You've lost weight too, haven't you? I thought your face looked thinner."

"Yeah, I lost over twelve pounds in two months, that's why I need the new clothes. And I have been painting up a storm, jogging and going to the gym again."

"Wow. What the hell is going on here? Whatever it is, I love it. Come on, let's go shopping before you change your mind."

They made a total of twelve stops for new clothes, shoes, gowns, jeans, hats, sunglasses, underwear, belts, bathing suits and everything else that Jessie thought was a "must have in a new wardrobe." They made a day of it.

They were nearing Sunrise Avenue when Jess said, "Make a right here and then the first left."

Katie followed her directions.

"Park anywhere. There's a spot, next to that van."

"Where are we going?" asked Katie.

"We are going to Jean Philippe's, the best hair designer in the city, bar none. If you are going to do all of this, it is time for a new haircut, sweetie. He is impossible to get an appointment with but I have been coming to him for years and besides I fixed him up with his current boyfriend."

Katie looked like a million bucks when she came walking out and she should have since the haircut, trim and style cost almost that amount. But it was worth it.

They had dinner at the Boca Hotel, overlooking the Inter-Coastal Waterway in Boca Raton and watched an old couple, dressed in matching green shiny outfits, glide across the tiny dance floor. It seemed to be no larger than the size of the dining tables but if you wanted to dance you took what you could get. They looked wonderful and they could not take their eyes off of one another.

"That is so romantic. We need to go dancing," said Jess.

"Yeah, find some guys and go dancing. Mickie would love that, I'm sure."

"He wouldn't mind. But let's not come here."

"Now that I have all of these new clothes, I have to find somewhere to wear them," said Katie.

"Hey, tell you what! Let me take you out for dinner on your birthday next week. My treat! We'll get all dressed up and you get to choose the restaurant. Next weekend we'll go out. It will do you good to get out. We can even go dancing at the J.W. Beach Hotel or somewhere else. Come on what do you say? What do you have to lose?"

Katie hesitated for a minute. "Sure, let's do it and I know just the place. I'll make the reservations for Saturday?"

"You bet."

After dropping Jess at her place. Katie stopped by her new gallery to walk through the refurbished building. It was coming along great. Permits had come quick, once they heard it was someone from Delray coming in to fill the space.

The blond hardwood floors, spot lighting, and white luminescent walls made the place a genuine upscale New York art gallery. That is just the look she wanted. She wanted a premium appearance to be able to charge premium prices. She would have an open house, once she had all of the bugs worked out. She was excited.

Katie pulled into her driveway, sad that she would be moving to a new place but happy that she would be able to live above her business. She loved short commutes. It was perfect. The space was so huge she had room for a large apartment in the rear and her art school in the front. After she showered, toweled off and dressed for bed, she read another letter.

May, 2008

My Dearest Darling,

I recall the yellow cotton dress, do you? Do you remember the first time we ventured to the beach? I always hated the beach, too sandy, too windy, too dirty and way too much trouble. You my love, reminded me of the beauty that the beach has to offer. You said the sand was once living shells, or coral or bones pounded by the relentless ocean into tiny particles of pleasure for us to enjoy to squish between our toes.

Remember you said we should treat it with respect as if it were a temple in honor of all those who had gone before. We should remember all of those living organisms that have given their lives to provide the soft, warm sands meant only to give pleasure to the soles of our feet.

Your eyes see things so differently than most, and when I think of the beach I think of us, so close and your appreciation of the world so profound, so human and so understanding. I love that about you, among so many other countless things which I adore about you, my love. I shall travel far but I am never out of sight of your love or your emotions, for I am always reminded of how you view the world. Bye my love. I must go.

Forever,

Jack

His darling loved the beach, he wrote in his letter, while he hated the beach. Katie hated the beach also, too dirty and sandy. The sand got everywhere. It took hours to clean up when she came home. And the small restaurant he wrote of, Cafe Luna, which overlooked the beach, she had passed by there many times but never stopped inside. She smiled, if he can try new things then maybe it was time for her to spread her wings again, to lift her veil and take flight.

Unbeknownst to Katie, dark glowing eyes outside watched as she walked inside her bedroom. He watched her dry herself and leered as she dressed for bed. The eyes gleamed in the moonlight, cursing at her.

"Patience," he said in a low growl, "patience." He moved closer, ever closer.

Chapter Seven

The movers emptied the last load of furniture inside the small beach bungalow in Delray Beach. Interior decorating was not one of Jack Petersen's strengths, so his sofa, desk, tall teak chest, vintage lamps and Moroccan prayer rugs didn't exactly go together, but that did not matter to him. With all of this around him, it now felt like home.

His son Danny had given him two new huge surf fishing rods as a house warming gift which he hung over the wall, arranging them so they formed a large X behind the sofa. Boxes of tackle gear, lures and assorted fishing paraphernalia, still in the packaging, were strewn about the living room.

"You will never go hungry living on the beach and having two fishing rods," Danny joked.

He brought some of his clothes with him but most of them he gave away to charity relying on his daily, never changing mainstay of tan cap, khaki shorts, white polo or t-shirts, sneakers and his old trusty Ray Bans. He gave Danny the responsibility of returning the trove of casserole dishes to their rightful owners back where he used to live.

Jack spent the last six weeks making the transition from his five bedroom house at the gated community of Bear Woods Country Club, to the small beach bungalow. He'd owned the place for six years but rarely used it over the past eighteen months, somehow never finding the time.

After his wife died, Jack would regularly be greeted by widows at his front door, bearing their best casserole dishes. They would make an impression, say hello, drop off the various dishes and then when it was time to return the casserole dishes to their homes it would be followed by another meal, wine and whatever would happen next. He missed his Laura more and more. Everyone told him time would make it better but somehow it did not heal the wound in his soul. He wanted to be with her.

Jack was not interested in furthering any type of relationship with any of the women and really just wanted to be left alone. One woman in particular was very aggressive in her push to make Jack her newest "friend." Her name was Virginia Coltart, who Jack called Ms. Tuesday because she would show up every Tuesday with a new casserole dish and a bottle of wine. She was quite attractive, nicely built and very wealthy, having divorced a magazine magnate three years earlier. She knew what she wanted and she wanted the good doctor as her next husband. Jack decided it was time to move.

The beach cottage sat low between two large grass and tree covered sand dunes, positioned with the intent to try to conceal the location of the small cottage. The house had originally been constructed as a caretaker's cottage for a large nearby mansion and guest house. It was over landscaped so that it could not be seen from the road, so as not to take away from the huge mansion it served.

The Gilders, moneyed people from Rhode Island in the electronics business, bought the mansion property, guest house and the caretaker's cottage. They next bought the mansion to the south of them and proceeded to tear down both of the two large structures. They planned to use all three lots to create a mega-mansion right on the beach. They intended to use the beach cottage as a building trailer and eventually level that as well.

After tearing down the two mansions, they applied for building permits and discovered the beachfront property had become a nesting ground for the endangered Florida Burrowing Owl. Construction ground to a halt. Later that year, a messy divorce awarded the caretaker's cottage to Rosemary "Marty" Gilder who promptly sold it to Jack and his wife so her husband could not build his dream "McMansion."

Jack filled the fridge with beer and some of the food he bought at the market and glanced about his new home. He had spent many nights there before he and Laura built their house and for some reason he felt closer to her here. This was now home.

"That's all of it Mr. Petersen. Take care now," said the potbellied mover who had the name Harry stenciled on his grey uniformed shirt.

"You want a beer or bottle of water to take with you?"

"Water's good," he replied, wiping the sweat from his balding head, with a once white handkerchief. "Can't drink on the job," he chuckled.

"Water's super cold. I put it in there a while ago. I'll get you one."

"Thanks Mr. Petersen. See ya now." And then he was gone.

Jack popped open a beer and went outside and sat on the small wooden porch which overlooked the ocean and provided shade during the afternoon heat. Inside the cottage was a large living room, a stone fireplace off to the right, flanked by his old comfortable sofa, and beyond that was a small eat-in kitchen. A small bedroom was at the rear along with a bathroom and shower on the first floor.

The larger second bedroom took up the entire upstairs, and overlooked the living room below, with a magnificent view of the ocean and beach. It was here that Jack Petersen set up his desk and computer.

Dr. John Petersen could well afford to hire a contractor to paint the place, fix the broken shutters, replace the railings on the front porch but to him it felt good to have a tool in his hand. It was not a scalpel or a surgical probe but rather a hammer, a screwdriver, or a paint brush but felt wondrous all the same. He had worked for many years for his uncle in the lumberyard as a teenager and he felt holding those tools again brought him home.

He looked down at his dark tanned hands, studying his long fingers with the blue veins traveling across the outstretched surface. His hair was longer than he normally wore it in the past. After he added some needed weight his face no longer looked drawn and haggard as it did during his ordeal. The crisp salt air, the long days outside and cool nights had done him a world of good, helped him get the rest he desperately needed.

The tall retired doctor grabbed his half finished bottle of beer and headed inside to set up his upstairs office.

Danny was a literary agent in Los Angles who did a lot of book and movie deals. "One step at a time," Jack would say when Danny started to talk about a movie deal for his book. He repeated the mantra every time Danny got a little ahead of himself, plotting movie deals and book signings. He reminded his son they needed to sell the book first, let it hit the bookshelves before they started planning anything else.

Standing in his upstairs loft apartment overlooking the ocean, he took in his accomplishments. It felt good to work with his hands again. He had painted the entire house, fixed the worn grey wood shutters, the long porch and refinished the floor inside by himself and the help of Danny.

He glanced at the picture of Daniel and his new grandchild, marveling at how much they resembled their grandmother. But it was time for Danny to go home, to be with his family, get back to his life. He picked up Laura's picture from the desk and smiled. God, how he longed for her.

The book was finished. Writing the book at least had brought some closure to his life's many loose ends. He was almost sorry it was over but happy to be have been able to work with Danny. He had missed him so over those years he was gone.

"Dad? Are you in there?" Daniel's voice boomed from the front door.

"Up here Danny."

"Dad, you left the front door open. Anyone could have walked in and stolen anything they wanted."

"Like what?"

"Well… well, like your computer, that's what."

"Let them have it. Danny boy, remember this is a beach house. One day it is here and the next day it could be gone, what with the storms, rogue waves, hurricanes and such. Life is like that. Remember?"

"Oh, you and your, 'remember', philosophy."

"That's just the way I am. Some habits are hard to break."

"I'm sorry, Dad. I wasn't thinking.

"You got any beer?"

"Yeah, I do as a matter of fact. Come on, let's chill out. Let me buy you a beer."

"Buy?"

"It s a figure of speech, Danny boy."

"I know that." Daniel glanced around appreciatively. "Place looks good and cozy, Pop."

"Yeah, that it does. Here's to my new abode. Cheers!"

"Cheers, Pop." Danny settled onto the soft sofa. "I returned all of the casserole dishes but I think the ladies were disappointed that it was me visiting them and not you. Oh, a lady by the name of Ginny said to give you hugs and kisses. Said she may drop by with a housewarming gift and visit once you get situated here. Nice looking woman."

"Yeah, just keep her away from me." Jack leaned back on the sofa.

"Okay, if you say so. How about I just send Heather out to visit you and bring the documents. You know, she had a thing for you. She drives all the guys in the office crazy. If I wasn't married, whew… I would give some serious thought to getting to know her better…, a lot better. If you know what I mean?"

"Yes, Danny, I know what you mean. There are girls like that in every office. Just remember you are married. You must have trust in a marriage for it to work, don't forget that son."

"Yeah I know, I was just saying if I wasn't, then… well, you know."

"Best not to even go there son."

Danny walked around the small cottage and noticed some boxes of books stacked in the corner of the small living room. "Dad, didn't you tell me you sold all of the books at the flea market last week?"

"Yeah."

"Then what are those boxes of books over by the wall there?"

"Well, I got rained out right after lunch, but I did sell all three boxes of your mother's books."

His son set the beer bottle down on the side table and walked over to the boxes pushed up against the wall.

"Wow," he said, "do these bring back memories. *Babson's Guide to Neurosurgery, The Physician's Desk Reference Book, Richards Medical Dictionary.* You kept all of these?" He tossed the large book over to his father. "I remember you poring over these when I was a kid, sitting beside you on the floor. Why did you keep them?"

"Sentimental reasons I guess." Jack took a drink from his frosty beer.

Danny began thumbing through some of the other books in the box. "This one still has a bookmark in it," he said, turning a page. "Dad! Look!" He held up a fifty-dollar bill. "This had to be Mom's doing. Hiding any cash she got." He opened another book and found another treasure. "This one has a one-hundred dollar bill in it."

Soon both men were on the floor carefully going through each book, searching for untold cash. Every other book held a fifty-dollar bill, a hundred-dollar bill or sometimes both. When they were done a tidy stack of green bills lay stacked on the floor.

"Count it up, Pop."

"You're the numbers guy Danny, I'll let you add it up."

His son began counting the cash and leaned back, taking a deep swig of beer. He whistled. "Three-thousand, one-hundred and fifty dollars. Wow, that's a lot of money."

"You better believe it."

"Dad, did you go through Mom's books before you sold them?"

"No."

"No? Not at all? Pop!"

"No, all I did is put them in the boxes and move them to the flea market."

"You gotta find them, fast. If Mom was putting this kind of money into your books can you imagine what she put into her books?"

"Yes, you're right! But I sold them and I don't know how to contact the gal I sold them to. All I know is her first name."

"Think Pop, think."

"She was very attractive, reminded me of your mother in certain ways. She did that funny little crinkle with her nose like your mom used to always do, remember?"

"Her name, Pop, what was her name?"

"I remember she said her name was Katherine but everyone called her Katie. Yes, that's it, I remember now. She told me she owned a secondhand bookstore either somewhere in Delray, Boynton Beach, or Boca Raton. That was the reason she bought all of your mother's books. Apparently romance novels are pretty popular."

"You've got to find her. And quick!"

"Danny, look, I have enough money for me to live any lifestyle that I choose. I don't need the money and neither do you, right?"

"Yeah, but Pop, Mom left it there for you. It was a gift from Mom. You have to find it. Okay? It was Mom's way of saying she was thinking of you."

"Okay, okay, if you say so."

"Dad, now you have to start checking for all of the secondhand bookstores and call them or go by and visit them."

"Danny, maybe they have already sold them. You know those kind of books are really popular. Did you ever think about that? I sold them, do you understand? I sold them, they no longer belong to me. I can't ask her to go through all of the books I sold to her and tell her to give me the money back." It just did not feel right to him. But on the other hand he would love to see her again. He was intrigued by her, she was different from the other women he met since his wife died. There was something about her. She had spunk and he liked that, he liked that a lot. That's exactly what had drawn him to his Laura. He smiled thinking about his late wife.

"I'll get the yellow pages and you can search for it on the Internet. Look under used bookstores and secondhand books."

"Danny, wait a minute. Let's talk." He moved to the sofa and motioned for his son to sit down next to him. "I appreciate everything you did for your mother and everything you have done for me. But it is time for you to get back to living your own life."

"I am, Pop. I am."

"Danny, go home to Cindy and the kids. I know they miss you and you miss them. I think you have spent enough time babysitting me. I will be fine."

"But Pop…"

"Go home. I love you, but it is time for both of us to get on with our lives. Go back to California."

"I have to be honest with you, I'm worried about you. Are you sure you'll be all right?"

"I'll be fine, son. I just need some time to myself that's all. Go. Go home."

"Okay, tomorrow. I'll leave tomorrow or the next day."

"Tomorrow, Danny. Tomorrow."

"Yes, then you can start looking for this woman named Katie and her secondhand bookstore. Okay?"

"Sure, whatever you say."

"Promise?"

"I promise you."

"Got any more beer?"

"Yeah, sure do. You know I have not had a beer in ages but for some reason it just feels right today." He walked back to the small kitchen and opened the fridge, all the while thinking of meeting up again with the pretty bookseller and her soft crinkling nose. *Yes, that would be good.*

Chapter Eight

Jack Petersen kept his routine when editing the same as when he was writing. He was up every day at five-thirty. After he wrote for an hour or so and then grabbed another cup of coffee and took his first break. He watched the glorious amber sunrise, peeking over the horizon to greet him and never failed to be awed by its magnificence.

He then wrote for a few hours more before taking another break to have breakfast and some more coffee. He would break later in the morning and go for a run along the beach. Watch the kite flyers, the fishermen and early beachgoers setting up their blankets and umbrellas for a day at the ocean. The kites looming overhead added to the festive air.

The sand felt cool to the bottom of his feet while the brisk salt air refreshed his soul. He had finished his last round of edits around four o'clock, about a week after his son left to return to L.A. He showered, and tried to decide whether to head down into busy downtown Delray for dinner or stop at his nearby favorite Italian restaurant on the beach, Café Luna.

Café Luna was at the end of busy chic Atlantic Avenue which dead ended at A1A. The restaurant was across from the beach, with indoor seating and outdoor tables stretched along the sidewalk under a broad green awning. They featured an entertainer on most nights, playing a soft guitar and the mellow music of Antonio Carlos Jobim. Jack liked it because they also served the best Northern Italian food in Delray. It had also been his and Laura's favorite.

Jack and Laura always asked for their usual inside table, number six. Even though it was inside, it was situated in front of the best window to watch the ocean vistas. It had the feel of the preferred outside table. Their preferred waiter, Tito, was the owner.

He had opened the restaurant fifteen years earlier and it became an overnight success. Great food, good service and his jovial always made for an enjoyable evening.

After he seated them, he would open the tall windows next to their table and if they listened real close, they could hear the ocean waves crashing just beyond the dunes outside. When dinner was over, the two of them would take off their shoes and walk along the beach, hand in hand. It was pure heaven. Tito's dinner did not disappoint him that night, even though Jack stared at the empty seat across from him, Laura's seat. God he missed her.

A few days later, Jack was running along the surf when an odd noise in the tall grasses, just off the beach, startled him from his thoughts. Following the sound, he heard a loud whimpering and discovered a mangled golden retriever puppy. He had white and gold strands of hair with big brown eyes. His rear leg looked as if it had been attacked by something. A shark? The pup lay there in the sand, weak and shivering, afraid to move. Jack stripped off his t-shirt, covered the puppy in it and hurried back to the cottage. He wrapped it in a blanket to keep him warm and stop the shivering while he tended to his wounds.

Jack surmised the puppy belonged to a boat owner and probably fell overboard and been attacked by an opportunistic shark before being washed ashore. It took four days before he finally showed some improvement and was up on his feet, as good as new. After that he followed Jack everywhere. Jack called him Duke after his Alma Mater. Tito became great friends with Duke and kidded Jack that he was going to kidnap the friendly golden retriever one day.

Just a week after sending Danny the finished book, his son informed him it was going to auction—publishers were excited about being involved. Danny had been sending out emails and letters to get the hype going before Jack had even finished the book. A couple days later, Danny sold it to the highest bidder. Jack liked his new editor, and was glad they wanted to keep it pretty much as is. They were eager to get it out on the market as well, and an early publication date was set. And now, just a couple months after selling, advanced reader copies had been sent to reviewers.

The phone rang in the bedroom, pulling Jack from his reverie. "Hello?"

"Hey Pop, I've got some great news for you. I'm sending the first copy of the book to you and preliminary reviews have been very good."

"Really? I was a little nervous but it felt good to write it. It brought some closure to a lot of things, if you know what I mean? Now I am done, all of my loose ends seem to have been wrapped up."

"I know exactly what you mean. I could not put it down, it was that good. And I would tell you if it wasn't."

"I'm sure you would, son, I am sure you would."

"Well the next step is a cross country tour, travel for some book signings, some lectures and speeches. You know what I mean? Then we can talk to the movie production people who review scripts for movies and made for TV movies. Remember, I told you they had an interest? But I will be showing it around to other places as well. Usually they like it if they can piggy back off a successful book tour but they liked the initial promo we sent, so we will see. Are you up for a book tour?"

"We'll see, Danny, we'll see. I don't want to make any long-term commitments, okay?

"What do you mean? Is everything all right? I detect some hesitation in your voice. And you don't sound like yourself."

"I'm okay, really. I just need some quiet time, you know, now that the book is done."

"Remember I told you what would happen once the book was published? Is there anything else bothering you I should know about?"

"I just don't know if I am up for making a long term commitment for a book tour that's all. We can talk about this later okay?"

"All right, but you are starting to worry me again. Are you sure everything is okay in Florida? I can swing by on my way to New York and we can have dinner if you like."

"It's just that the anniversary of your mother's death is coming up again soon. It kind of gets to me Danny, that's all. I miss her terribly. But, I'm okay, really."

"Hey Pop, I got an idea. Why don't you come out here for a visit, to California? See the grandkids, do grandpa stuff; you know we would love to see you. What do you say?"

"Sounds very inviting. We'll see, all right?"

"Okay, but if you need to talk, I'm just a phone call away. Call me. Okay?"

"Yeah, okay."

"Promise?"

"I promise."

"Hey speaking of promises, how did you make out finding the used bookstore woman? You promised me you would track her down. Have you had any luck finding her? And what's going on with you and promises? I have never known you to break a promise. I think maybe I better come out there and see what is going on."

"I will start looking for her tomorrow, for sure, I promise. Good night Danny. I love you."

"Love you too, Dad. Goodnight."

Jack sat on the front porch with Duke. They watched an offshore lightning storm light up the evening sky. "Hey boy, how do you propose we track down this lady and her used bookstore?" Duke licked Jack's face before laying his big head onto Jack's outstretched feet, making himself comfortable.

"We start looking tomorrow for this woman named Katie. Right boy?" The growing and contented puppy fell sound asleep at his feet. Jack watched the offshore pyrotechnics as it illuminated the cool night air. Magnificent, he thought, before turning in for the evening. "Tomorrow," he promised.

Chapter Nine

Katie moved the large storage bookcases in her apartment out of the way, over to the side wall. She used the oversized shelves to store extra copies of books she had accumulated and now, the cleared area was to be her new, temporary studio.

She drove to the Artist Corner, the nearby art store which was closing its doors, and she stocked up on everything she needed. She bought small and large canvases, paints by the carton, brushes, artist's knives, palettes, easels, frames, drop cloths and everything else she would need and could fit into her SUV. She had lots of space that she could use top store everything.

The re-energized artist would always start the same way. She would close her eyes, take a deep breath and envision the letters from Jack in her mind and think about how the letters made her feel. She would think about what he was going through when he wrote them, and then she reopened her eyes and began to paint.

Katie at first painted with a timid soul until she became bolder. The brush would sweep from side to side as if it were music released from captivity. Soaring high, the expression came from within her minds eyes and then reflected onto her canvas. The result was wonderful and magical.

In her paintings, it was as if her dam of emotions had broken and now washed over the blank cotton canvas. She almost felt there was a hand guiding hers, as it became a work of art, transforming a blank desert into a wonderful insight into her fertile new feelings. Swirls of color, passions of purple, reds, yellows, and ambers singing loudly to be released from where they had been imprisoned. It seemed somehow the melody of her soul transformed the painting, her hand began to move without her direction, joining the passion which filled her mortal being.

When she finally finished her work, after painting for hours without stopping, she would slump back into a nearby chair, exhausted. She viewed her work as an outsider and saw the internal message in her tribute to Jack. The letters had now become her guiding light but her life was becoming fuller and richer as she expressed herself so completely in her work. She stood naked in her emotions before him, not ashamed, not withdrawn but content. She loved painting more than she had remembered and was tireless in her new efforts.

Katie turned over the day to day operations of the bookstore to Donna, who loved books, loved the store and loved the customers. After the first couple weeks of running the store, Donna approached Katie with the largest smile Katie had ever seen.

"I want to buy the business, Katie. I love it."

"You just bought yourself a bookstore, Donna! I hope it brings you as much joy as it brought me."

Katie painted for hours and then sometimes days on end, at times not even stopping to eat or drink anything. It was usually at the urgent insistence of Felix that she would pause long enough to feed him and let him outside.

When the paintings were finished, she leaned the canvases against the side wall to dry. Each painting was different and they each whispered a special story to Katie, while she would stand there to admire them, listening to them tell their special tale. She was pleased with her work.

The determined artiste would begrudgingly take an occasional break to inspect the ongoing construction of her new emerging studio and apartment besides she was running out of art supplies and paint.

Her new space was undergoing a complete transformation from a former furniture store to a hip, chic art gallery. She had the passion to paint but she also knew she had to oversee the business aspect of her gallery.

Katie made another foraging run to the Artist Corner and wished the owner well as she loaded up the SUV and decided to have lunch before returning to her studio. She stopped at Momma's Madness Organic Restaurant on Atlantic and ordered an early lunch. They had the best tofu salad and they made their own pesto on the premises.

She began to look through her punch list and realized she was far behind, as usual, when suddenly she had an uncomfortable, eerie feeling of being watched again. She looked up and noticed the restaurant was completely empty. But across the street she could make out a lone figure, standing beside the huge Banyan tree which shaded the city square. It was homeless Sidney. He must have followed her from her apartment to the restaurant. She thought she had seen him earlier, lurking by the drugstore off of Third Street.

The thought of the creepy old man just standing there, watching her, gave her chills over her entire body. When the waitress brought her lunch Katie was distracted for a brief moment and when she looked up again, he was gone. Maybe it was just her imagination. Maybe she didn't really see him after all.

Katie unloaded the paint supplies from her SUV and carried them upstairs to her apartment. She could not help but look anxiously around the outside of her building, to make sure she had not been followed, again.

She waved at Donna as she passed by the front of the bookstore heading for the rear stairs of her apartment.

"Hi Katie, how's it going?" Donna asked from the porch, closing the glass front door behind her.

"Behind schedule of course," Katie replied, "but I will pull it out on time I'm sure. How are you doing?"

"I'm having a great time and have started some children's programs to bring in the mothers and their kids more often," she said with a big smile.

Katie noticed, for the first time, Donna had on a t-shirt and a pair of nice fitting, hip hugger jeans, a big departure from her usual long black dress uniform that Katie was accustomed to seeing her wear.

"I do a reading for them every morning," she continued, "and it gives their mothers time to browse through all of the books or just have a coffee, get together with their friends while they sit around the sofa. They love it and it has increased sales. I am thinking about doing it twice a day, starting next week."

"Fantastic! Good luck with it. I know you will do well," Katie told her as she lifted the box.

"Oh, Katie one thing. I did want to tell you that creepy Sidney has been by just about every day asking for you. I know he's harmless but he still just gives me the willies. I thought you should know about it, that's all. Have a good one!" Donna waved her hand and she walked back up the steps into the bookstore.

Katie gave her conversation with Donna a troubled thought while she grabbed the last of the boxes and headed upstairs. Her attention was soon focused on other matters. She would have to start packing for her move as she thought about her new life.

She closed the upstairs door to her apartment but she did not see the old, red Ford pickup truck drive slowly by. The brake lights shone but for a brief moment before it drove off, making a u-turn at the corner out of sight and parking in a secluded area down the street.

Chapter Ten

Jack finished his morning jog, with Duke running behind him, snapping and chasing the growing number of seagulls who lingered on the beach before scattering with his yelping and playful snips. *He wouldn't know what to do with one if he caught one,* Jack thought amused by his growing puppy's behavior.

He grabbed his coffee mug, an English muffin with orange marmalade and headed upstairs with the county phonebook tucked under his arm. He set it on the desk and opened his notebook. "Let's see," he said out loud to help him think. "Fact one, she said her name was Katie, short for Katherine." Second, he remembered she said she owned a used bookstore. Three, she said she hoped to see him in Delray, Boynton Beach or Boca Raton. So her store was probably in one of those cities.

"Hmm. What do you think, Duke?" The golden haired dog was on his feet, ready to go for another jog, panting, tilting his head to the side, with a questioning look on his face.

"Duke boy, we just went for a run. Lay down and let me finish here, then we can go outside again." He did an Internet search for used bookstores and then secondhand books, then antique books for Delray, Boca Raton and Boynton Beach. He hit search and thirty-eight responses came up.

"Whew," he said, as he printed the list. He next pulled out the phonebook and looked up used books, secondhand books and anything else he could think of in the book business. There were over twenty listed in the yellow pages and cross checked them with his computer list.

As he looked over both lists he realized he was looking forward to seeing the woman named Katie again. Instead of calling up the various shops on the list, he decided to visit them in person. He methodically went through the list and picked the ones that were on his route for the day.

"Come on boy," he said to Duke, "let's get some fresh air and run some errands." After visiting ten bookstores, no luck. No Katie.

Figuring the book business was a tight knit group of people and they would all know one another, he asked each one he stopped by to see, if they knew of a bookseller named Katie. No one did, but most of the booksellers he talked to had been in business only for a couple of months. Apparently there was no long term job security in the secondhand book business. Over the next three days Jack stopped by or called over twenty-five bookstores. No luck.

Since there was still some daylight left, he had time to check on one more bookstore. The next one was called, Second Hand Rose. He drove through Delray and turned off the main street, heading towards the trendy Pineapple Grove District. The old building which he stopped in front of was sheltered by two huge mahogany trees, providing cool relief from the hot mid-day Florida sun.

He crossed the name off the list and walked up the creaking grey painted steps. Jack peered into the store through the front window, placing his hand over his eyes to block the refection on the window. Then he saw it, his medical reference guide on the top of one of the shelves— *The Surgeon's Guide to Thoracic and Cardiovascular Surgery* by Doctor John Petersen.

This had to be the place. Who else would have his book on their shelves?

He looked inside again and went to reach for the door before stopping. He could now say he found the store, just like he promised Danny he would. He would just tell Danny there was no money. Let her keep it, she could probably use it more than he could. But, he thought, it would be really nice to see her again.

I'll just pretend I was in the neighborhood and just passing by. A large black and white cat jumped on the counter inside of the store and lay down, wrapping his tail around his body. Jack looked through the large widows and could see no one inside.

Finally, he grabbed the doorknob, and turned the old brass handle. It was locked, they were closed. It was then he noticed the front door sported a low slung sign hanging from a string in the center of the glass door. It announced the store was closed and would reopen at nine a.m. the next day. *Too late.* He walked back down the well worn wooden steps to head home. *Goodbye, Katie,* he said to himself. *I guess it just wasn't meant to be.*

Chapter Eleven

Jack Petersen was awakened from a dead sleep by the sound of Duke barking and scratching at the bedroom door, trying to get out. Duke always enjoyed their early morning runs along the beach before breakfast, even though his gangly legs caused him to run faster to keep up with Jack's long limbed trot.

Sometimes Jack's long haired companion would just stop and sit along the water's edge as if to say he had enough but he was always game to start again. But today was different, his pleadings were more urgent than ever before.

Jack heard a rumble in the background, and the cottage shook. It was not thunder, to be sure, his awakening mind registered. More mechanical, having a steady noise, raising and lowering in volume and pitch. Jack threw on an old pair of beach shorts, his Blackbeard Ale t-shirt, slipped on his sneakers and made his way downstairs past the wheezing coffee pot. Is that what was making all of racket? He studied his ancient noisy coffee pot. Then he heard it again, closer this time, like the thunder of a jet roaring directly overhead.

He went to his front porch, only to be confronted by a construction crew using a bulldozer about to start leveling the protective dunes around his home.

"Hey," Jack hollered, trying to be heard over the din of the huge mechanical monster, which at this moment was lifting truckloads of sand in one huge scoop of its massive shovel. The enormous machine billowed blue and black smoke from its exhaust high over the head of the machine operator as he backed up to make another run at the defenseless and devastated sand dunes.

Jack waved his arms frantically over his head, and stood in front of the massive earthmover. "You can't do that," he finally said quietly, after he forced them to stop their machine so they could hear what he was saying.

A man in a blue work shirt and hardhat approached him. "What's the problem here?"

"You are on my land," Jack told him defiantly. "I want you off my land, now. Cease and desist." The man was joined by the bulldozer operator and two other men in suits, who had been standing and watching nearby. The men in suits came closer to see what the problem was.

"What are you, a lawyer or something?" asked the first man. "Cease and desist? Normal people don't talk that way."

"I want you off my land, now. And leave my sand dunes alone. "

"Well sir, Mr...?" asked the blond haired man in the tan suit, with a skinny face ending in a pointy chin as he peered at him through thick glasses perched at the end of nose.

"Petersen, Dr. John Petersen. I own this land. I have owned it for the last fifteen years and I want you and your work crew and your equipment off my land or I will call the police."

"Well sir, I have a permit here from Palm Beach County Permit Office to begin our development on this land. We are building four condo buildings with over five hundred condos total."

"Not on my land you aren't."

"Mr. Petersen, did you not get a notice of eviction? It should have been posted on your front door over two weeks ago."

"I hardly think so. I have been here every day for the last six weeks."

"Mr. Petersen, I'm sorry," said the other man in the suit. "The land was deemed abandoned because of nonpayment of property taxes to Palm Beach County Land Assessor. That's what the tax office decided and we bought the property at an auction in tax court," said the other man.

The tall man, who joined the group was round at the belly, had jet black hair, which obliviously had been dyed, given the light roots, with matching dark eyebrows and a brooding face. He was dressed in an expensive dark navy pin striped suit. He was clearly the ringleader of the group and since no one in Florida wore dark suits, he had to be from out of town.

"Sir, the taxes on this property have all been fully paid, in advance every year, automatically through the Florida American Bank & Trust," Jack told them.

"Well, you will have to look into that and see what recourse you have through them Mr. Petersen, in the meantime we are behind schedule. We will give you one day to clear out your things. We will be back tomorrow to continue our development of the property."

The man in the dark suit paused for effect, to make his point before he continued. "You, Mr. Petersen, will be arrested tomorrow by the Sheriff for trespassing if you are found on my property. Do I make myself clear?" Without waiting for a response from Jack, he turned and walked away, joking with the man in the tan suit.

"Yes, perfectly." Jack's eyes narrowed for a fight. "Excuse me! Excuse me! I do have a question."

The man stopped and paused before turning around. "Yes, Mr. Petersen? What is your question?"

"I was under the impression that this land was protected under the endangered species act and was not eligible for development because it is a Florida Burrowing Owl habitat."

"I don't see any owls here now…, do you, Mr. Petersen? I didn't think so. Good day, sir."

"Excuse me! Excuse me! What is your name?"

The man stopped and this time did not even bother to turn around to face Jack, he merely said out loud in response, "Scarlari, Mr. Victor Scarlari." He then kept on walking.

"Mr. Scarlari," Jack said to the big man walking away, "the name is Petersen, Dr. John Petersen." Jack turned and walked away, leaving Scarlari in the sand, puffing on his large Dominican cigar.

"Watch him," Scarlari said to the big man walking next to him named, Thomas "Tommy" Malone. "He could be trouble. This project is too big for any trouble. Do you understand me? Huh? *Capiche?*"

"Yes, Mr. Scarlari. I'll handle it. Don't worry."

Scarlari stopped and turned, his dark piercing eyes bore deeply into the man. "I'm not worried Tommy. If anyone should be worried it should be you. It's up to you to make sure nothing screws up this up. You got it? And I mean nothing. This is a three-hundred million dollar project."

"Yes, sir."

Jack walked back into his cottage, his mind already making up a plan to try to save his home. He started making phone calls. He was not leaving his property.

Eyes followed him into his cabin, peering inside, watching him from the cottage window.

Chapter Twelve

Katie woke early to oversee the set up and check the final construction punch list for her new gallery and apartment. She had a lot to do if she was going to open on schedule. She passed her confidant, Jack's medical book, and said, "We are going to miss this place aren't we, Jack? But you are going to love the new place, just you wait. I will see you later." And she winked at the book.

She was going crazy working with the crew of craftsman who seemed to be running in and out, all who needed direction and, of course, payment. It was crazy but a good crazy and she loved it.

Katie had electricians, plumbers, lighting people, security folks, the phone company, the utility companies, the bank, painters for final touch ups, and the sound company to wire it all together. In addition she had to deal with the flooring company, the carpenters, and of course curious customers knocking on the door trying to get in to look around.

When they took a break for lunch, she decided she could use a break herself. She walked down Atlantic Avenue and grabbed a latte from a nearby coffee shop. It was sunny outside that afternoon but cooler under the trees that lined the street. She reached into her purse and unfolded one of Jack's letters to read.

October, 2008

My Dearest Darling,

I heard a laugh the other day and it brought back memories of us. Remember the time we decided to bake a cake and spent all that time waiting for it to rise, only to discover we had forgotten some key ingredients? Your mother was kind in her suggestion for us to take up skydiving instead. We laughed for years anytime we would order cake for desert.

Your laugh would start from the corner of your lips and spread upward until it reached your emerald green eyes, causing them to twinkle. You had different laughs for different times. Your laugh with me came from the depths of your soul, seasoned with sweetness and tempered with respect and trust. I miss that laugh so much my love.

Remember your aunt, so good, so proud and so giving? I recall it was at your sister's wedding. Your aunt was returning from the ladies room, her dress tucked so neatly inside the top of her undergarments. You laughed until you cried as she walked across the dance floor, unknowing.

I was left with the unenviable task of using my jacket as her privacy shield, while she adjusted her clothes. Remember? She did not speak to you for weeks. But I still remember your laugh from that evening. Laugh today. Laugh tomorrow. Laugh until you cry. Laugh often. Laugh as if we are together, for I miss you so. Always remember…

Must go my darling.

Forever,

Jack

Katie did not know whether to cry or laugh after she finished reading the letter. She was glad that she had saved the letters to read one at a time. Her initial reaction was to read them all at one sitting but the letters replaced her box of chocolates and she read as she needed them. The letters were just as fulfilling as her wonderful Belgian chocolates but with considerably less calories. As unlikely as it sounded, she was falling in love with this wonderful, sensitive man she knew only through his letters.

She finished her coffee and went back to the gallery to supervise the first delivery of artwork and sculptures. This was going to be big she thought to herself. She was going to display not only her pieces but others that she thought were good and deserved recognition. Grand opening was in two weeks. She could hardly wait.

That night she fell into bed without undressing, dead tired. She was exhausted from the constant running and the only thing that kept her going was her adrenaline rush. But the gallery was coming together faster and better than any of the ones she'd created in the past. She was back on schedule but she did not have the energy to do anything else. It was two a.m. Lying in bed, she felt a chill come over her as if someone was watching her. She went to the window and closed the seldom used drapes before returning to bed. There was no one living behind her so she had complete and total privacy. But she could still not shake the troubling feeling.

Outside her building, dark eyes waited, lurking, hidden by the overcast trees. He was unfulfilled. He gritted his teeth and cursed at her for closing his view. The sound of rustling leaves filled the air. He cursed her under his breath. "Enough of this. Your time is now." He crept to the rear door and turned the door handle.

Chapter Thirteen

The bulldozers started their engines right on cue at seven a.m., sending dark smoke curling high above the machines. Soon the wistful clouds were caught by the early morning sea breezes, twisting them and dissipating them into a puff of nothing.

Jack grabbed his coffee mug, followed by his trusty guard dog Duke who stood by his master, a low growl lingering on his lips, hanging onto his tongue. He thought himself ferocious as he stood behind his master to protect him.

"Quiet," Jack whispered hoarsely to Duke. "Behave yourself." Silence followed, as Duke walked beside him.

"Morning," Jack said to the operators, as they shut down their machines and sat with arms folded, awaiting some direction.

"Listen mister," said the older operator, "we don't want any trouble. We are just workin' stiffs, you know?"

Tommy stood by his car across the street and began to walk towards Jack and his dozer operators, accompanied by a uniformed Palm Beach County Sheriff's Deputy.

"Morning," said Tommy. "You were ordered off this land yesterday by the land's proper owner and you were told you would be arrested should you remain. This is the sheriff's deputy Allan Fox here to perform his duty. Officer, arrest this man for trespassing."

The young officer reached behind his back to retrieve his handcuffs just as a State Police cruiser pulled in front of Jack's house. He walked toward them and handed Malone a document saying, "I have a cease and desist order signed by State Judge Howard Kirk ordering all parties to appear before him in court to show just cause in two weeks. All construction activities are hereby halted. Gentlemen, please immediately remove all construction equipment from this property."

It was only a temporary reprieve. Jack had to get to the bottom of what really was going on. Something was terribly wrong.

• • • • •

The Boca Raton branch of the Florida American Bank & Trust was a short drive down I-95 on Glades Avenue, the main, palm lined thoroughfare in this upscale town. Boca was noted for expensive cars, high-end shopping, and upscale businesses.

The branch itself was located in the lobby of the ten story FAB&T high rise building, with blue tinted mirrored glass wrapping the building. Inside, the modern structure was cool, a welcome relief to Jack as he made his way across the plush burgundy carpet.

A pretty young greeter approached Jack as soon as he walked into the branch office. "Can I help you, sir?" Her voice was pleasant and she smiled a broad welcoming grin.

"Yes, I would like to see the manager please. I believe his name was Morton, James Morton."

"Yes sir, I would be happy to arrange that. And your name, sir?"

"John Petersen. Your bank does the tax processing for my property in Delray Beach."

"Yes, Mr. Petersen, I will have you speak with the new manager, Mr. Burns. You see, Mr. Morton no longer works for the bank." She picked up her phone and placed a call before quickly returning her attention to Jack. "If you will follow me, Mr. Petersen. I will take you to see Mr. Burns." The young girl was a blonde, whose swaying rear end matched the rhythmic swing of her ponytail as they walked to the large manager offices.

"Mr. Petersen, welcome." Mr. Burns smiled broadly leaving his chair from behind his modern desk. His wooden nameplate centered on his desk proclaimed: *Robert Burns - Branch Manager*. Yes, Jack was speaking to the right person.

"Have a seat, sir, how can I help you?" The smile never left his face.

"Well, I think there must be a mix-up somewhere. Can you pull up my account on your computer, please Mr. Burns?"

"Yes, sir. I would be happy to. All I'll need is a photo ID for verification purposes, you understand?"

Jack smiled as he handed over his Florida driver's license.

"Let's see," Burns said as he typed in the needed data. "Ah, here we are, Dr. John Petersen. I see you have a rather large account with us, you are a Silver Platinum Customer, we auto service your property taxes on the property located at 301b North Ocean Drive."

He continued to read as he scrolled down his screen. "I see also you have a checking and two saving accounts and four rather large CD's, and a brokerage account with us. We really appreciate your business, sir. How can I help you?" The ever present smile never deflated from his face. Jack could guess Burns did not come into contact with that many Silver Platinum account holders and had been told to give them the bank's special customer service.

"When do you show the last payment was made for the property taxes on my house?"

"Let me see," he said, punching in some strokes on the keyboard. "The last payment was made January 15th of this year, over six months ago. According to our records, the transfer was completed and you are totally up to date, Dr. Petersen."

"Well, I just had some people come to my house yesterday and said the house was auctioned due to non-payment of property taxes. How do you explain that, if, as you just told me, the taxes were paid on time?"

"Well, well, ah… Dr. Petersen. What I said was the transfer was made and I assumed the payment was delivered to the Tax Assessor's office."

"What does that mean? I don't understand."

"Well, Dr. Petersen, we are a very large bank and this service is provided as a courtesy to our best customers. Since you have no mortgage on the property and own the property free and clear, it is something that we do not do for everyone. You see we contract out this service to a servicing company who handles making these payments." The smile drooped and was now a half-hearted effort. His forehead was spotted with tiny beads of sweat. "I can assure you, Dr. Petersen, we have never, in all of the time I have been with the bank, had a complaint against the company who handles this for us."

"Can you call them and ask them if the payment went through?"

"Of course, Dr. Petersen," Burns replied, the smile reappearing on his face. The speed dialer sprang into action and was soon followed by muffled conversations from the other end.

Finally, Burns said into the phone, "This is Bob Burns, branch manager at the Glades branch of FAB&T. Ma'am, I am looking to have confirmation that the property tax payment went through on property #384589PB-8493L-9830-RC-9349. Was the payment made?" He paused. "It was?" He gave Jack the thumbs up sign. "Can you send me your confirmation sheet from the County? I would like to have it for my files. I would also like to provide my customer with a copy."

Way to go Bobby! Bravo! Jack thought.

"Well if your fax is broken, I would like to ask that it be messengered to us. Can you arrange that please, Melissa?" He covered the mouthpiece of the phone and asked Jack, "They are just around the corner from here, it should take no more than fifteen minutes to get here. Would you like it messengered to your home or would you care to wait for it here?"

"I'll wait here," said Jack. He could listen to one side of the conversation and pretty well figure out what was going on.

"That would be great," Burns said. "I'm sorry, your name again? Melissa. Wonderful. Thank you for your help, Melissa. The customer is waiting here. Great! Then your messenger should be here soon. Fifteen minutes. Wonderful, thank you so very much for handling this so quickly."

A big smile of victory returned to Burn's face as he shook Jack's hand. "She said it will be here in fifteen minutes. You can make yourself comfortable in our client's lounge if you like. There is coffee, soda, water, bagels, newspapers, a TV, and the like."

"Thanks for all your help, Mr. Burns. By the way, how long have you been with the bank?"

"Since the beginning of the month. Why do you ask?"

"No reason, just curious. Thanks again for your help. Oh, what was the name of the servicing company?"

"South Florida Servicing Corporation on Lyons Road. But it should not take long at all, Dr. Petersen."

The fifteen minutes stretched into an hour and Jack returned to Burns' office, who had another customer with him. Burns waved and picked up the phone, presumably to call the service company and inquire about the delay. *That's what I like,* thought Jack, *good follow-up. But this seems to be taking way too long.*

After ninety minutes passed, Jack closed the *Sports Illustrated* he'd read three times and headed for Burn's office once more. It was empty. The blonde, twenty-something at the reception desk smiled and said, "Mr. Burns is out to lunch. He'll be back in two hours after his appointment. Can I help you with anything?"

"Yes, you can." Now it was Jack's turn to force a smile and turn on the charm. "Can you write down the address and phone number for South Florida Servicing Corporation on Lyons Road. They were supposed to messenger something here and it never showed up. I am running late for an appointment, so I thought I would just go by there and pick it up."

"Sure! I can even give you directions on how to get there. I pass their office on my way home."

Jack started up his old, tan Mercedes and immediately lowered the windows in the hot, oven-like car, while cranking up the air-conditioner to the max. He bought the car new years ago and he just could not bear to part with it. He had it serviced every year and it still ran like new, even with one-hundred thirty-thousand miles. People joked that it was still in its break-in phase for a Mercedes.

Jack drove down Glades and made a left onto Lyons, following the blonde's written instructions. He soon left the high rise office buildings, past the one story industrial courts until he came to a low rent mixed residential and office area. He glanced at the sheet of paper she gave him and realized he'd passed it. Turning around he saw the address, 359 South Lyons Road on the side of a low slung, grey building. It was a two story, non-descript office building. He parked his car out front.

Jack walked inside and checked the directory for their suite #202 and got off the elevator on the second floor. He made his way down the poorly lit corridor and soon he was standing in a dingy reception area. A sign was posted on the wall which merely listed the initials, SFSC, Ltd.

"Hi," he said to the older woman behind the reception desk.

"Yessss," she responded ever so slowly, glancing over the top of her reading glasses to examine him.

"I would like to talk with Melissa. Mr. Burns, from FAB&T was waiting for a document for me but since it has been over an hour I thought I would come over here and pick it up." He heard a cough and looked behind him. An elderly man was sitting reading a magazine.

"I'm sorry sir, were you next? I did not mean to jump up in line."

"No, I'm waiting for Mrs. Forester," he replied.

"Yessss," she said again, this time more impatience evident in her voice.

"I would like to see Melissa."

"You'll have to wait a minute. Please have seat. What's your name?"

"Petersen, Dr. John Petersen."

She picked up the phone and shortly thereafter a frizzy red-haired young woman, wearing an unusually ugly dark plaid blouse, came from her behind her cubicle.

"Yes," she said with a sniffle. "I'm Melissa. How can I help you?"

"Melissa, I'm Jack Petersen. I was with Mr. Burns in Boca at FAB&T. I was waiting for a copy of the property tax payment receipt from the County you were to send over with a courier, remember?"

Her eyes suddenly grew wide in recognition, finally putting together the face and the name.

"Oh, yes," she stuttered and proclaimed the obvious. "He never showed? " she asked in false bewilderment. " I am so sorry, I am going to have a talk with him when he gets back. Have a seat please, Mr. Petersen. I will run off another copy for you."

She left but was back ten minutes later to ask for his address again. He could hear loud but muffled voices coming from behind her cubicle. He could not make out what they were talking about but they sounded like they were arguing in a rapid-fire manner. Finally, Melissa came out from behind another cubicle with an envelope in her hand and gave it to Jack.

"Sorry for the delay, Mr. Petersen. Will there be anything else?" She sniffled, her apparent allergies acting up.

"No that will be all. Thanks." In the elevator, Jack pulled the document from the manila envelope and saw immediately it looked like a cut and paste job and a poor one at that. He could make out the edges from where they had copied it and then pasted it over some other document and then made another copy. It did not look real and he was not buying it.

He stopped on the ground floor to look over the document in more depth, glancing at the building directory. The name at the top of the directory said simply, The Scarlari Building.

Jack examined the building registry and he could pick out at least three different companies listed, all with the Scarlari name associated with it. Now he had a pretty good idea of what had happened. Scarlari was behind it all. He really wanted his home. Well, he was going to have to do more than that to take Jack Petersen's home, a determined Jack told himself.

Chapter Fourteen

Jack made multiple trips to the bank and various Palm Beach County offices and found everyone to be exceptionally helpful and friendly. He was finally told he needed to see the head assessor for his appeal to be of any help and soon found himself sitting in front of Bernice Bertram, Head Assessor. A plumpish, middle-aged woman, dressed in a light colored blouse, a flattering skirt and a nice smile.

"I wish I could help you, Dr. Petersen," she said, leaning forward in her chair, speaking in her most sympathetic voice. "But the payment was never received by our office and we did try to notify you on numerous occasions by mail. Unfortunately, we had to post a sign on the property that it was going up for auction. I'm sorry, there is nothing more I can do. I wish I had better news for you."

"Where were the notices mailed to Mrs. Bertram?"

"Well to the servicing company of course."

"Ms. Bertram, I appreciate you taking the time to see me but you are my last hope. I never received those notices."

"Call me Bertie please," she said with a knowing smile. "I just don't know how I can help you."

"I had the bank tell me the payment was made. I also went directly to the servicing company and they told me they paid the taxes. And I have a copy of the receipt from them showing it was paid to the County."

"Really? May I see the document receipt please, Mr. Petersen?"

"Sure."

"What is the name of the servicing company?"

"It's South Florida Servicing Company. Why?"

The woman leaned back in her chair while she examined the document. "Hmm," is all she said, as she examined the document closely. "We have had some issues with them over the past few months. Nothing I can go into now but let's just say, some issues."

"Bertie, I have been living at the beach property every day for months and I have never received any notices from your office in the mail and I certainly never saw an auction sign posted on my door."

She set the paper on the desk and pulled her computer keyboard tray close to her. "You got this document directly from them? They hand delivered it to you?"

"Yes ma'am, I was right in their office. A young woman named Melissa gave it to me."

"I see now where the problem may be coming from. All of the notices were sent directly to the servicing company, including our default and auction notices. It sounds as if they never forwarded them on to you."

"That's right. Finally we are getting somewhere."

"Well, yes and no. In the State of Florida, I must submit this information to the County Attorney General's Office to review and investigate. He then will make a report and recommendation to the State's Prosecutor for his follow through determination." She removed her glasses which had been perched precariously on the end of her nose before continuing. "They will have a hearing on the case and you may be called to testify at that point and then the Prosecutor will make his recommendations. If he recommends a criminal prosecution and is successful, then and only then will you have your relief and be able to keep your property."

"Bertie it is not only my property but it is my home. It is where my wife and I spent many precious moments. Times I will always cherish as my fondest memories. Anything you can do to help would certainly be appreciated." He stopped and feeling defeated, he asked, "How long will all of this take?"

"If we are lucky and everything goes smoothly, I would say sixteen to eighteen months."

"I don't have that kind of time. I have a hearing due soon on the true ownership of my home."

"I'm sorry Dr. Petersen but there is nothing else I can do."

• • • • •

On Friday, the courtroom was crowded for the weekly hearings. Men in suits conferred with their clients, mothers pulled their unruly children outside to discipline them and lawyers were everywhere watching the proceedings unfold. It was like a circus, with so many people coming and going. Jack felt he was just one of the main attractions.

Jack was listed on the docket as the third case to be heard before the honorable Judge Kirk. He'd spent the last two weeks doing his research and building his case but had very little to show for it.

I just hope I have enough time to stop this. His thoughts were interrupted by the booming command from the bailiff, "All rise for the Honorable Judge Howard T. Kirk, presiding. This court is now in session."

Behind the judge's chair, the door opened and a tall distinguished man dressed in a long black robe strode into the courtroom. He walked up the three small steps to a podium and sat in his large green leather high backed chair which provided him a grand view of the entire proceedings. He first looked over the courtroom with a wide sweeping gaze until they landed on the rear of the hearing room when he locked eyes with Victor Scarlari. Jack saw the recognition, the pause and nothing else. It seemed to Jack he was the only one to see this subtle communication. After watching this interaction he knew the fix was in and he had little hope of achieving his goal of keeping his house. The judge was there just to make it official.

"Mr. James Richmond, please address this hearing."

An elderly man hobbled towards the front of the room, leaning from one side to the other. He stopped in front of the platform to address the judge. It was very noticeable that he could not stand straight but rather leaned dramatically to his left, probably the result of back surgery gone horribly wrong. He wore a tattered baby blue shirt that had seen better days, splotched with multiple stains across the front, and down his old trousers.

A skinny little man, wearing oversized glasses was seated at the rear of the courtroom. The man rose and walked towards the other lawyers stand to present his case against the elderly Mr. Richmond.

"I is Jim Richmond, Your Honor."

"Mr. Richmond your property was foreclosed and was purchase at auction by the Sun Company. It is all perfectly legal, Mr. Richmond."

"Your Honor, being legal don't make it right... do it?"

"I am sorry, Mr. Richmond, this is a legal proceeding not a confessional. You will have to move on, sir."

"But, Your Honor, my family has lived by that water for as long as I known. It's home for me and my kinfolk. I pays my bills on time. I don't know what happened, I's just don't know. Where we's go to live, Your Honor?"

"Next case," said the impatient judge.

The bailiff led the old man to the rear of the courtroom. He was still mumbling incoherently to himself, "I justs don't know. I don't unnerstand this," he continued to mutter, as he walked past Jack, sounding so bewildered.

Jack watched the man leave through the back door of the courtroom and saw the skinny lawyer representing the opposing side return to his seat at the rear of the room. He sat down and conferred in a huddle with the man sitting next to him—Victor Scarlari. *Seems like Scarlari has his hand in everything,* thought Jack.

"Robert Walker, can you please step forward," boomed the bailiff again to the waiting group in the courtroom.

A young man in a tennis shirt and shorts stepped forward. "I'm Robert Walker, Your Honor." Scarlari's attorney again made the pilgrimage to the front of the courtroom and took his place at the other podium representing the new owner at the hearing.

"Your house was foreclosed on for non-payment of taxes and was duly auctioned by the County Tax Office for such nonpayment. Do you have anything to say?"

"Your Honor I never received anything from the County or the Assessor's office saying I was delinquent. I know I would have noticed something like that, I know it, Your Honor." The young man sounded desperate.

This does not look good.

The Judge handed the bailiff a document to give the man to review. "Mr. Walker, this document was sent to your home advising you of non-payment on your property taxes and the possibility of it going to auction. Is that your name on the document?"

"Yes, Your Honor, that is my name, but I have never seen this document. Honest. I have not."

"Auction stands. Next case."

The young man leaving the podium was dumbfounded. "I don't know what I am going to tell my wife," he said, in tears. "We sank our entire life savings into that house. It was supposed to be our beach house getaway. Our nest egg, gone. No, no, I can't believe this, I can't believe it." He walked away sobbing.

"Petersen, John Petersen, please step forward." Jack rose and walked to face the judge from the podium across from the familiar face of Scarlari's attorney standing next to him.

"Mr. Petersen, this document was sent to your home advising you of non-payment on your property taxes and the possibility of it going to auction. Is that your name on the document?"

"May I see the document, Your Honor?"

"Yes, you may," said Judge Kirk, slightly perturbed to have his routine altered. He handed the paper to the bailiff, who passed it to Jack for him to read.

"If that is your name and address, Mr. Petersen, than I am ready to rule on this case."

Jack gripped the paper in his hand, sudden relief filling him. His name was spelled wrong on this legal document. Thank God! It was a slim hope but it was all he had.

"Your Honor," interrupted Jack.

"Yes, Mr. Petersen?" The judge was now clearly agitated. "That is your name on the document, is it not? That being the case I find that…"

"Your Honor, that is not my name," Jack said to the startled judge.

"What do you mean it is not your name? It clearly states it was sent to Mr. John E. Petersen. Is that not your name?"

"No, Your Honor. That is not my name. My legal name, for all legal documents, is John A. Petersen not John E. Petersen. That is clearly not my name."

"You are right, Mr. Petersen," said the old judge, making a furtive glance to the rear of the courtroom. "Notice of intent is hereby repealed and this document must be re-filed. Mr. Petersen, you can't help it if the wrong name is on a document. I will see you back here in a thirty days, Mr. Petersen," said Judge Kirk, sounding more like a perturbed high school principal than a nonbiased legal arbitrator.

Jack passed the chair of Victor Scarlari who did not even look up from his heated discussion with his attorney. Jack could tell he was not a happy man.

As Jack left the courtroom he did not notice that Scarlari's right hand man, Tommy followed behind him at a discreet distance. Tommy knew where Jack lived but all the same he was going to follow him. He had his man in his sights. He knew his next steps.

The next morning Jack woke with Duke at his feet, sound asleep. *Great guard dog you turned out to be.* The big dog growled at an imaginary intruder in his sleep while Jack tip-toed downstairs and grabbed a cup of coffee, before walking out on his porch to begin his day. It was there Jack found a large black and white poster stapled to his front door. It contained only one sentence, *EVICTION NOTICE, Palm Beach County.*

Pain radiated through Jack's chest, this is one thing he did not need, especially now. Scarlari had declared war, but it didn't matter. Not now, not anymore, not as far as Jack was concerned. He knew what he had to do. He was busy the whole day and it was late when he finally pulled into his driveway. A car passed, pulling to the side of the, before taking off again. He was being watched.

Chapter Fifteen

"Hello?" said the groggy voice into the phone at midnight. Psychologist Judy Goodeheart lay in bed, knowing no patients would call her at home this late. She also knew her two kids were already snug in their rooms and hearing Pat's snoring noisily next to her she knew of only one other person who would call her.

"Hello sis, how are you? Is everything okay?" she said without opening her eyes. Maybe it was a dream or a wrong number.

"Hi, Jude. Sorry to wake you but I really needed to talk to someone. If you're asleep, I can call you back tomorrow. I'm sorry."

Judy, always available to lend a helping ear to her sister or anyone else for that matter, sat up in bed and cradled the phone on her shoulder next to her ear, speaking softly so as not to awaken her sleeping husband.

"Who is it?" queried the sleepy voice next to her.

"It's Katie. Go back to sleep."

"Hi Kate," said her sleepy husband, not bothering to move and very familiar with the late night calls from his wife's younger sister. That was the last noise from him until his usual snoring began anew.

"Sorry, sis. I know it's late but I really needed to talk to someone."

"It's okay. I'm awake now. What's going on?"

"I don't really know where to begin." Katie sounded nervous.

"Start at the beginning," counseled Judy, plumping up her pillow, anticipating a lengthy story. Pat snored again beside her.

"I went to one of my flea markets and met a man there," she began.

Judy was immediately awake and listening. "Yes, and what happened?"

"Well he was really good looking and was selling some used books his wife had accumulated before she passed away. When I got the books home I found money in a couple of them but I also found a number of love letters inside, all signed by him." She paused. "These love letters were so romantic and so personal, I felt like I was reading someone's diary. It was spooky. I almost felt like I was intruding or something on the guy's privacy. You know what I mean?"

"So what's the problem? You read some love letters a guy wrote to his wife and you feel guilty? Is that it?"

"Well yes, but, I love the guy's letters and I'm finding we share so much in common. Never mind. Go back to bed. I should have never called you. It's late. It's crazy."

"Katie? Katie, I'm here. Talk to me."

"Well, I love the guy's letters, they are so romantic and so personal, he loves this woman so much, it is unbelievable."

"I thought you said she was dead?"

"She is, but she was alive when he wrote the letters to her. But he could have written the letters to me the way he writes. You know?"

"Don't tell me you have fallen in love with a guy because of the letters he wrote? Is that it? That is it, isn't it? Katie, you are such a romantic. You need to get a grip, do you hear me? You need to get on with your life, Kate. You are transferring your feelings for Richard onto this guy. Move on and forget about Richard and this letter writer."

"Jack."

"What?"

"His name is Jack. I met him, remember? Would you like me to read you one of the love letters he wrote? No, I better just let you go back to sleep. I'm sorry I woke you."

"No, no that's okay. I'm awake now. Read me one of his letters." Judy heard the rustling of paper on the other end of the line and when Katie returned to the phone she said, "Here goes," then taking a deep breath she began.

November, 2008

My Dearest Darling,

I saw a bird, a large white bird soaring overhead today and it reminded me of the seagulls we used to feed on the beach. Whenever I touch my wedding band, not only does it remind me of you but reaffirms this magical connection between us.

Remember our wedding day? We were determined that no one would separate us, ever, and we held our hands clasped so tightly together no one could pull us apart. You always said how a couple spends their wedding is how they spend the rest of their marriage. We spent ours together! I always tell everyone it was the happiest day of my life.

Do you recall, we recited verses to each other quoting from your old friend, Elizabeth Barrett Browning? Her verses were our wedding vows and the tears streamed down your cheeks as never before. Remember our vows my love? (I left out the first line which you hated so, thinking it overused.)

I love thee to the depth and breadth and height
My soul can reach, when feeling out of sight
For the ends of Being and ideal Grace.
I love thee to the level of everyday's
Most quiet need, by sun and candle-light.
I love thee freely, as men strive for Right;
I love thee purely, as they turn from Praise.
I love thee with a passion put to use
In my old griefs, and with my childhood's faith.
I love thee with a love I seemed to lose
With my lost saints, — I love thee with the breath,
Smiles, tears, of all my life! — and, if God choose
I shall but love thee better after death.

I can't believe I remembered the whole sonnet! But my joy over our wedding was only surpassed by the birth of Danny, our wonderful son. I miss him more than hearts can tell, as I miss you my love.

Remember at our wedding, your uncle Frank and Aunt Eileen wanted to grab us and pull us apart to meet some out of town guests? But our hands and hearts were locked together. It was a grand time. I mean it when I say it was the best time of my life. I still remember your wink as you walked down the aisle with your father. You looked so prim and proper before blowing me a kiss and then smiling your gorgeous smile. Oh god, do I love your smile. I had to chuckle to myself, walking down the aisle after our vows, you could not stop whispering your new name. Remember?

I am so glad I married you.

Forever,

Jack

"Well, what do you think?" There was silence on the other end of the line as Judy weighed her words, brushing aside the tears after hearing the letter.

"Katie, that was so incredibly romantic! This is the sort of thing that *all* women dream about, someone who puts them first, someone who speaks to their inner self." She paused to recall the wonderful words she had just listened to and reached over to caress her sleeping husband before she continued.

"I was lucky enough to find someone who treats me this way. Most men *barely* remember their wedding anniversary, maybe because they're trying to forget that they're married at all. They hardly remember their wives or their responsibilities." She paused for a moment longer to compose herself. "Maybe that's because they still want to be footloose and fancy free. Most men are still kids at heart and not in a good way! So, to have a man write something like this, so profound, so warm, so embracing, this is every woman's fantasy."

"So what do I do?"

"The way I see it Katie, you have one of two choices. You can let it go or you can go for it. There is nothing in between. Don't wait; don't let life pass you by. What is the worst thing that can happen? You find him, you don't hit it off or he still feels married to the memory of his dead wife and he breaks your heart. That is not as bad as what you are living through now. Go for it! Okay? And if we are done I am going to lean over and kiss my husband and tell him how much I love him. Good night, Katie. I love you."

"I love you too, sis. Thanks. Sorry to wake you. Goodnight."

Katie lay back down on her bed, the words from her sister still ringing in her ear. *If I ever see him again, I know exactly what I will say. Yes, I know exactly what I am going to say.*

Chapter Sixteen

The phone rang on his desk across the room but Jack let the annoying ring continue until it finally stopped. Minutes later his cell phone on the wooden bedside table rang. *It must be Daniel.* He did not feel like talking to anyone today.

Tomorrow was the anniversary of Laura's death and he was not in the mood to talk with anyone, not even Danny. He finally swung his feet off the old iron bed and let them land on the hard wooden floor, threw on some swim trunks and went for a swim.

The ocean was cold but refreshing, with the waves crashing and massaging his body, the salty spray flying high into the air. Everyone should have an ocean at their front door. Duke was content to lay and watch by the shoreline, until some pesky seagulls piqued his interest and off he went on a wild chase.

Jack knew he should make an effort to find out what was behind the eviction notice posted conspicuously on his front door. He knew he should also investigate the whole property tax matter. Today was not the day. Time was running out.

With Duke on his heels he jogged for thirty minutes before heading back to his cottage. He showered, changed, ate breakfast and was out the door to begin his errands.

Jack parked behind Doc's Pharmacy after tying up Duke at the doggie pole and filled a nearby water bowl for him to drink from.

"Hello, Dr. Petersen, how are you, sir?" asked the cheery pharmacist, Joe Boots.

"Good except I have not been sleeping real well here lately. Can you tell me if you have this in stock?" He handed the pharmacist his prescription.

"I think I do, Doc. How many do you need?"

"Eight to ten tablets should do it."

The pharmacist looked at him strangely before saying, "You know this is a controlled substance. I will need a second doctor's signature on any prescription."

Jack pointed out the two signatures to the white haired pharmacist behind the prescription counter. "Look there Doc."

"Well everything seems to be in order. But I must warn you, take no more than one every ten hours and under no circumstances should you take more than one or use this medication in conjunction with alcohol. Okay?"

"Got it."

"I'm serious Doc, dead serious. This is some heavy duty stuff. This stuff can kill you especially if you mix it with alcohol."

"Got it. I'll be very careful but I think I know what I am doing."

"I know Dr. Petersen, I'm sorry. Of course you know but so few of these scripts are written because they are so powerful." The old pharmacist looked somewhat embarrassed, his face flushed, as he lectured the renowned Dr. John Petersen. "By the way, this prescription expires in two weeks. You'll have to go back to the other doctor and have him co-sign for a new prescription."

"It is a little dated. It was written almost a year ago when I had a really hard time sleeping. I don't think I will need a refill or new prescription, but thanks for the reminder."

Jack finished up the rest of his errands and stopped by a local convenience store along the way home to purchase a bottle of wine. A nice white Viognier, one he could chill in his fridge and then sit on the front porch of his cottage and drink while he watched the reflections of the setting sun on the ocean waves.

He fed Duke and later walked along the shore, thinking of, wishing of so many things in his life and soon he found himself back at the cabin. He uncorked the wine and counted out six sleeping pills on the kitchen counter, then put them in his shirt pocket.

The sun was beginning to droop as he settled into his favorite deck chair where he had the best view of the ocean waves. He loved watching the waves crash methodically onto the sands, splashing, foaming as they made their way onto the beach only to return to the sea to begin all over again.

He sipped the wine, it was cool to his mouth, sweet but refreshing and the coolness glided down his throat, tracing its path to his stomach. It tasted very good this evening. He reached inside his pocket and retrieved the six rose-colored pills that would bring him closer to Laura.

Jack took another sip of wine and was joined by his daily companion Duke, laying his big head and floppy ears onto his lap, looking up at him with those big brown eyes. He forgot about Duke when he made his plans. Not every plan is perfect but he stopped and thought about his options. He would have to make up a story and leave him with someone, someone who would take good care of him and he knew just the person. The rest of the wine would have to wait.

Chapter Seventeen

Katie spent the day inspecting the building, testing the lights, the alarm, the sound system and anything else she could think of in advance of her grand opening. The paintings were breathtaking for she included some of Atherton's finest modern impressionistic paintings, art pieces from Chargan, one large bronze sculpture by Berezina and six of her own paintings which together filled the gallery. The lighting was perfect. A few passersby tried to open her front door.

"Friday," she told them through the glass door. "We are opening on Friday. Please come back." Katie waved at them, amid smiles and their thumbs up signal wishing her luck and she knew she was on her way.

Katie sent out invitations to all of the art critics at the local newspapers, to the four major South Florida televisions stations, to all the big and small interior decorators, and many other key people she knew would have an impact. She planned to have waiters in tuxedo circulating through the gallery all evening with wine, cheese, shrimp and other hors d'oeuvres. She hired a violin player to stroll through the gallery, playing classical music throughout the night.

Everything was set. At least that's what she hoped—she'd said the same thing the night before and then found twenty other items which needed her attention. But tonight she and Jess were going out to dinner and would enjoy themselves. After dinner they would go to the JW Beach Hotel and watch people dance or as Jess would say with her mischievous smile, "Maybe find someone to dance with or whatever."

Katie rushed home to get ready for the evening. She had been looking forward to it ever since Jess first mentioned it weeks ago as she glimpsed herself in the mirror and toweled off from her shower. She was pleased with what she saw, her new haircut made her feel younger, her body had lost it chubbiness and the tone had returned to her muscles. Her chest was still firm for her age, as she spun around in front of the full-length mirror, humming an unknown tune.

Tonight she was going enjoy herself, because tomorrow the moving van was coming to move her things to her new apartment over the gallery. *Lots going on.*

· · · · ·

The stalker stood in his favorite location at the rear of the building, deep in the shadows of the protecting brush and overhanging Banyan trees. It was the perfect peeping location. He was hidden well in the deep overgrown brush which lined the rear of the property. His cold dark eyes watched her every move from the shadows below. He'd gotten scared off the last time he was here. But not this time. He would not wait any longer.

· · · · ·

Kate dressed quickly and glanced in the mirror before grabbing her car keys, admiring her new look. She loved the stylish new shoes, the sleek skirt and the soft shimmering silk blouse with its sexy feel. All together they made her look and feel like a million bucks. She spun around again and then she was out the door.

The air was still warm but cooling down, as she drove east on George Bush Boulevard, turning south onto to A1A, in hopes of missing all the downtown traffic. As she drove down her favorite stretch of road, the ocean was on her left with its huge mansions and gated entrances. Most homes were hidden from view by huge private landscaping, tucked away, back from the street. Katie loved this drive down the coast.

She drove along the ocean with the sun low in the sky. The wind gently blew against the palm trees that lined the scenic byway. It was acres of green with colorful flowers everywhere she looked. Katie was mesmerized by the waves coming in, pounding the beach, splashing the water high in the air against the beachside rocks before receding again out to sea.

Kate loved these kinds of evenings, still warm but she knew she would need a wrap later as the night breeze cooled the evening air. There was a gentle wind riding the salt air, it smelled so good, as she breathed deeply. Approaching the commercial district, people started to appear along the sidewalk cafés as she neared Atlantic Avenue.

The young valet in front of Café Luna restaurant took her car, slowed and did a double take as she walked away, admiring her. She was pleased she had passed the test, the *look* test. She looked smashing even if she did say so herself. The ten outside sidewalk tables were already full with evening diners.

It was a beautiful evening to enjoy outside but an errant storm could pop up in South Florida at any time with no one the wiser. She preferred the inside table at the café, table number six.

She stopped at the outside reservation podium. "Good evening, ma'am. Good to see you again. Do you have a reservation?" said Tito, the owner, who was wearing two hats as usual that evening. He was the greeter and waiter for the inside tables until the rest of his help arrived.

Kate had lunched at Café Luna a few days before *and* this was the restaurant Jack wrote about so fondly in his letters, always asking for table number six. She enjoyed it on many different levels.

"Good evening, Tito. How are you tonight? I have a reservation for two, table six, for seven o'clock, the last name is Kosgrove."

The white jacketed maître d', with the ever friendly smile, responded quickly, "Of course, Madam, I remember you from lunch the other day. Welcome back. Table six is very popular but I did reserve it for you, as requested. Please follow me."

She walked inside behind him. The bartender waved and greeted many by patrons by name, the bar area being full with the regulars ordering their usual drinks. In the corner, off to her right, a guitar player sat on a stool tuning his instrument, getting ready to perform. Tito took her inside to the first table in the second room overlooking the outside tables just beneath hers.

"Here you go, Madam, table six just as you requested. You were best to reserve this table since it is one of the most popular tables in the restaurant. Let me open the windows for you, the breeze is wonderful tonight and if you look beyond the dunes you can see the sailboats rushing to get in before sunset." She could see now why Jack liked table six so much. When she visited at lunchtime she had sat outside at one of the sidewalk tables but this was the right table for tonight, she thought to herself.

"Thank you, Tito." She watched the sailboats in the distance, with full sails, leaning into the wind, making windward time but doing it so gracefully they appeared to be standing still.

The small restaurant was already busy and it was not even prime dinner time yet. Soon, waiters and waitresses hustled by coming from the kitchen. The room was so small they hoisted the large hot platters of aromatic dishes high above their heads and made their way around the restaurant, past her table, to those waiting patiently outside. The walnut paneling inside had mellowed to a golden shade of brown and the columns, covered in mirrors, made the room appear larger.

"Can I start you with a glass of wine?"

"Yes, Tito, I'll have a glass of Chianti and some bread with your wonderful garlic and olive oil spread. No, I changed my mind, make it champagne. I am celebrating my birthday tonight."

"Happy birthday, Ma'am! Yes, indeed. I will leave a menu here for you and one for your friend. I will be right back with your champagne."

"Thank you." She was early but she knew she could always count on Jessie to be on time. Opening the menu, she perused the daily specials. The warm bread and baked garlic quickly appeared and Kate marveled at how large the garlic cloves were. They melted in her mouth. You could use the cloves like butter they were so sweet and soft. The bubbles from the champagne tickled her mouth, before rolling down her throat.

"Tito," she asked, as he walked by. "What is your recipe for making this garlic taste so wonderful and sweet?"

"Family recipe, ma'am, I cannot share, so sorry."

"If I guess, will you tell me if I am right?"

He was up for the challenge. "Sure," he said, folding his arms with his towel draped over his hands, grinning.

"Well, it tastes baked, it is not a usual garlic because it is too large, probably made from elephant garlic. Right so far?"

"Correct," said the Tito an amused smile.

"Probably wrapped in foil, baked with salt and pepper and olive oil drizzled over the top?" Tito smiled and nodded in the affirmative.

"Very good, Madam."

"But what gives it the sweet flavor?" she asked out loud, tasting the garlic spread one more time. She was stumped.

Tito leaned over beside her, and whispered in her ear, "Limoncello. I put just a splash of Limoncello over the top, but I bake it in parchment paper not foil. But very good, Madam, very, very good."

Tito walked away humming. He liked this new visitor, she reminded him of someone. Just then, the door opened revealing his favorite customer, Dr. Petersen. Jack came in with Duke in tow and handed the leash to Tito. He had called him earlier to make arrangements for him to watch Duke ... for a few days.

"Tito, I really appreciate it. I am traveling this week and I am sorry it is such last minute thing and such short notice."

"No problem, Dr. Petersen. Me and Duke here, we are old friends. I like him and he likes the fresh veal chops I feed him. Right Duke, old boy?" Duke barked and broke free from the leash.

• • • • •

Kate was getting hungry and Jessie was fifteen minutes late, very unusual for her normally punctual friend. Just then her cell phone rang, loud enough to attract the attention of other nearby patrons in the restaurant. She searched inside her purse which was lying on the seat beside her and scrambled to answer it. Peopled stared at the intrusion.

"Hello?"

"Hello, Kate? It's Jess. I'm on the way to the airport. The hospital just called and said my Aunt Sophia has suffered a heart attack." Her aunt, who lived in Chicago, had practically raised Jess after her mother died. They were very close. "I am grabbing the nine o'clock flight out to Chicago. I'm going to have to take a rain check to celebrate your birthday. No dinner and dancing tonight. I am really sorry, Katie."

"Jess, that's okay. How's your aunt? How is she doing?"

"Not good, the doctor was not hopeful so I am trying to get out there as quick as I can. I'll make it up to you Kate, somehow, I promise."

"Don't worry about me. Go take care of your aunt. Call me and let me know if there is anything I can do, okay?"

"If you can go by my place and feed Matey for me until I get back, I would really appreciate it. His food is in the fridge, as usual. Thanks Kate, sorry but I gotta go. I'll call you when I know something." Matey was Jess's pet blue Macaw, which she treated like a member of the family.

Kate was concerned about Jessie's aunt but had to admit she was also feeling a little let down. She had to spend the evening by herself, after getting all dressed up and looking forward to it.

Well, you have a choice, she said to herself, *you can go home feeling sorry for yourself and finish off the gallon of chocolate ice cream or have a nice glass of champagne, a great dinner and watch the boats sail by.* She made up her mind…, she was going to stay.

"Tito, I'm ready to order," she said, raising her hand motioning to Tito, to flag him down. She watched Tito chasing, then holding onto a friendly but rambunctious dog. The lanky golden retriever came towards her and licked her once, then again as Tito was trying to restrain the friendly dog.

"I'm sorry, I will be with you in just a moment. Are you not waiting for your friend?"

"There will be just one this evening, my girlfriend will not be making it tonight. I'm afraid I'll be dining alone." She smiled in spite of herself, determined to enjoy herself tonight. Her mouth dropped as she saw him standing there behind Tito. It was Jack!

"Katherine? Is that you?" Jack, *the Jack,* stood right in front of her.

Chapter Eighteen

Jack stood back, helping Tito restrain the now wild and rambunctious dog, with Tito holding the leash. He was just as she remembered him. She gazed at him, but words refused to come. Words she'd practiced to say when they finally came face to face. She had memorized them for weeks, and now, they were gone in an instant. It was him, but she could not move, she could not talk, yet there he was, just as she always dreamed. Jack, standing right before her. She gaped at him, not believing her eyes. It was truly him.

Say something girl. Don't look like a complete fool.

"Katherine? Katie? That is you. I hardly recognized you. New haircut? You may not remember me. We met briefly at the Atlantic Flea Market. I'm Jack, Jack Petersen." He stood there in an awkward silence, she said nothing in response. *Maybe it was a different woman.*

Of course she remembered him but the words were stuck in her mind not traveling to her lips. *God help me push this boulder from my lips and help me say something, anything. Please!*

She finally forced the words from her mouth, "Oh yes! Hi... Yes, I do remember you. The doctor with all the romance novels, right?"

"Yes, that's me," he said, relieved and extend his hand to her. His hand felt large and firm but warm to the touch, not soft like she thought a doctor's hand would feel. "I was just going to do carry out tonight since they were so crowded. I could not help but overhearing you are dining alone tonight?" he paused before continuing, not really sure what to say. "Would you like some company for dinner? May I join you?"

"Of course," she responded enthusiastically, finally recovering from her trance-like state. "Please have a seat. Where are my manners?"

"They are pretty full here tonight," he said, making small talk. He pulled out a chair from the table. "There are no tables available that's the reason I was going to do take home." He smiled and her heart melted. He quickly added, "Sorry for my dog, Duke. He is a little excitable."

Tito started to walk away, with Duke following close behind him, licking his tongue panting for his expectant pork chop, expecting he would be fed some of the finest veal available. "I will take good care of him for you while you are away, Doc. Trust me, he's in good hands. I'll be right back."

Jack settled into the seat across from her. She could not help but gaze at him, remembering the letters, the words he wrote, so sweet, so warm, so romantic and so touching. It was as if she, Katie Kosgrove, a lucky fan, was with *the* rock star that everyone wanted to be with. She dreamed of this often and now it was coming to pass. She was giddy, like a school girl.

"Would you like another champagne Ma'am," asked Tito as he poured a glass of water for Jack.

"Thank you but I'll take a Chianti instead please, Tito," she responded.

"Champagne? Special occasion?" Jack asked.

"Yes, it's my birthday. I was waiting for my girlfriend, but her aunt suffered a heart attack and she got called away to be with her. You remember Jess from the flea market?"

"Oh yes, I remember her. She was pretty unforgettable, the way she pushed between us" Jack said with a grin.

"We were going to have dinner and then go over to the JW, listen to the music and watch them dance."

"Well, if I may. I would love to buy you dinner, as a birthday gift to you. No obligation, of course.**"** He spoke the same way he wrote, with a gentle and calming choice of words. So sincere.

"I would like that." Katie began to relax. **"**I would like that very much," she repeated, smiling at the man who sat before her. A man she thought never to see again.

"Settled then." Jack smiled, before leaning back in his chair, appearing to be completely relaxed.

"A glass of wine, Dr. Petersen?"

Jack opened the wine list and closed it in one easy motion, "I don't know why I bother to look at the wine list, I know just what I want. Tito, I'll have my usual. Bring me a glass of—"

"*Sangiovese,*" said Katie, finishing his sentence.

"Yes, exactly," said Jack, looking at her strangely. "How did you know I like *Sangiovese?*"

Heat rushed to Katie's cheeks as she remembered reading of Jacks affection for the Italian wine he loved. She'd read it in his letters.

"You seem like a *Sangiovese* kind of guy, that's all, Dr. Petersen," she said hastily.

"You are amazing, Katie. But it is Jack, please call me Jack."

"Okay…, Jack."

"How did you make out with all of the books from the flea market? Hopefully you were able to use some of them. My late wife had very eclectic tastes."

Katie took a deep breath and decided now was the time to come clean and tell him about all of the love letters and the money she had found in the books. She did not really want to tell him that she had read them, but if he asked she would tell him she read one, only one.

"Everybody loved the books I got from you. But, I am glad that you mentioned them." She took another deep breath before proceeding. She realized the time to tell him was now or never. "When I was going through the books I found some things in them that I think belong to you. I would like to return them." There now she'd said it. It was out in the open and she would give him the letters back and start fresh with him. They belonged to him. He should have them, even though the ones she had read did have a magical effect on her.

"Katie, I have given it a great deal of thought," Jack said having made a decision that she could probably use the money more than him. "I even came by your bookstore one evening but it was closed. I decided then, that I wanted you to keep whatever you found inside."

"You do? Really? Are you serious?" Katie asked. She had a hard time understanding his feelings on this as her face contorted slightly as if to question him but decided against it. *If they were my letters I sure as hell would want them back, yes I would.*

"Yes, I am. You bought the books so they belong to you and anything you found inside belongs to you. I want you to keep the money. Do you understand?" *I like this lady,* Jack thought. From meeting all the bookstore owners in his search for her, he'd discovered they all seemed to be struggling. *Let her keep the money. She could probably use it more than him.*

"Yes, but Jack what about the…"

"Katie I really don't want to talk about it anymore, if that's okay with you. They were my wife's books and I am glad you could use them."

Panicked, she didn't know what to say, she had to tell him about the letters. Later, she would tell him later. Now just smiled at him sitting across from her.

Oh God, I hope she doesn't think I am patronizing her. Best to end this while I am still ahead of the game and she doesn't think I am a jerk. Jack grinned nervously at her as he waved to Tito to take their dinner order.

Katie fiddled with the napkin on her lap, stalling, thinking of how else to ask him without embarrassing him. His response bewildered her.

"Are you sure about this Jack?" she whispered. To her the letters were priceless. *She would never give them up, at least not that easy. Oh my God, maybe he doesn't know about them?*

"Yes, I am sure. Enough of found treasures! Can we please change the subject? Tell me now mind reader, what do you think I should I have for dinner? Guess what I have an appetite for, Katie?" he asked her as Tito approached the table to take their order.

Katie picked up the menu again and looked it over twice before saying to the most attentive Tito.

"Hmm… Tito, how about the Saltimbocca, with orzo? A Caesar salad and some more baked garlic and fresh bread, if you please."

"You are amazing! That is exactly what I wanted. How did you know?" Jack exclaimed.

"Jack that was easy, they are the best items on the menu." She teased him in a most flirtatious way, a huge grin on her lips. *Those letters sure were coming in handy.* She heard the waves crashing on the beach beyond them.

"Look," she said, gently touching his arm, "look beyond the dunes! See the sailboats? They were tacking to the East now to the West. They look so beautiful don't they? Their sail so full of wind, like a rooster puffing his chest. Beautiful! And the fishing boats chugging behind them."

"Yes, they do. Do you sail? Or fish?"

"No, I always wanted to learn. I was a kind of a tomboy growing up, if you know what I mean. "

"Where did you go to school?"

"I went to Brown University in Providence Rhode Island. I studied Fine Arts, which is funny since I grew up a tomboy, but my mother insisted."

"Funny, that is where my wife went to school. Then she went to Yale Nursing School in New Haven."

"Small world isn't it, Jack?"

He looked at her, thinking, *Who is this woman? Why didn't I stop back at her store and talk to her? It was closed. Why didn't I go back there? Dummy me.*

"Yes and getting smaller all the time. How is the used book business, Kate?"

"I am not really sure. You see, I sold the business to one of my best customers, a lady named Donna McIntyre. I am opening an art gallery right on Atlantic Avenue. I am so excited, I can't wait. My grand opening is on Friday."

"Wow, really?" Jack asked in amazement. *This woman is full of surprises.*

"Yes. Donna kept saying she loved the business so when I decided to open the gallery she was the first one I approached about taking over my lease and the inventory."

"Wonderful! I guess? Do you know anything about the art business?" Jack asked quizzically.

"I used to own and operate a number of art galleries in New York. I sold the stores after getting married and invested the money. When my divorce went through, I wanted a change and decided to move here. I love books but, I also love art and I missed it, the creative side of it, the painting and the sculpting."

Katie's enthusiasm filled the room and Jack could tell by her sweeping hand motions and exuberant smile and laughter that she had found her true passion. He found himself urging her on.

"What do you create?"

"I love to paint abstract impressionism and I am enthralled by modern sculpting. I also love to take budding artists under my wing and nurture them and plan to open an art school, just like I had in New York."

Katie's chest puffed full of excitement and she felt like she was floating on air. He was so easy to talk to she did not want to ever go home. She wanted to just sit there and talk with him all night. She glanced at Jack and smiled, still not believing he was there, in the flesh. On an impulse she blurted out, "Jack, why don't you come for my grand opening on Friday? I would love to have you there."

Jack suddenly paused and thought of this evening and what he had done before coming here. He thought of the pills lying on the counter and the wine bottle at home. He did not believe in fate, or karma, but he did believe he had met this woman tonight for some reason, why he had no idea.

"Jack," she asked again, jolting him back to reality.

"Sure," he said quickly, agreeing but not believing his ears. "I would love to. Did you come from an artistic family? Did love of the arts come naturally? Where did you grow up?"

"My mom was into the arts but she owned a ranch outside Big Sky, Wyoming and my dad worked in New York City. We spent most of the time in New York but Big Sky country gets in your blood and you never get rid of it."

"I love it out there." Jack smiled.

They talked the night away, like old friends. They laughed together, him with his effortless smile and rolling laughter. His hand sometimes brushed hers, ever so slightly when reaching for something on the table.

"Do you read a lot?" he asked, "I mean, you having been in the book business."

Here's your chance to bring up the letters again. Maybe he misunderstood me. No, I am not going to say anything again.

"I love to read. I read romance, poetry, the classics but I am more an artist."

They talked about Florida, sports, politics, religion, immigration, love, relationships, talking non-stop.

She reminds me of Laura in so many ways, thought Jack. *Her easy ways, her burst of laughter, her serious frown, the crinkling of her nose. Yes..., she reminds me of my Laura.*

When they stood to leave, Katie stumbled on a step and he caught her, she brushed against him, touching his arm and shoulder. She could feel the firm muscles of his arm under his soft cotton shirt, while she traced the subtle lines of his biceps with her fingers. They walked outside into the cool Florida evening, and she pulled her black silk wrap snugly around her. There was a slight chill in the night air coming off the ocean breeze.

At the valet stand, he turned to her, smiling and said, "You had mentioned dancing. Would you like to go to the JW across the street, have a nightcap and maybe dance? Or watch them dance?"

"Well, I'm not much of a dancer but I love to watch them dance the Rumba. Sure, why not?" She grinned, her night was getting better and better.

The inside entrance of the JW Beach Hotel was decorated with dark wooden paneling which had a casual elegance to it, adding to a mellow glow from the nearby lights. The grille room was just off the large ornate lobby and a three piece Latin trio played soft, mellow and melodic songs. Katie and Jack grabbed a table by the dance floor and ordered an after dinner drink. They listened to the beat of the wonderful music and watched two couples dancing on the floor.

"They dance well, don't they?" Katie mused. "I would love to learn how to dance the Rumba one day."

"Follow me." Jack said, standing and held out his hand, leading her to a small area out of sight of the dance floor. "Let me teach you the Rumba. It is very easy." His voice was so calming.

Jack took her hand into his and struck a dance pose, standing straight, knees slightly bent, his arms drawing her ever so close. He was much stronger than he looked with his broad shoulders towering over her. His grip was firm but not overpowering. The mere act of being this close to him made her knees weak.

Toughen up girl, she said to herself, *if you want to get anywhere with this guy. You are going to have to control yourself.*

"Katie, think of the basic step as a walking around a square. You have two basic moves, to the side and then forward or back. Once to the side, then back, then to the side then forward, then to the side then you just continue to repeat the steps. That's the basic."

It sounded so simple when he explained it to her. She'd taken lessons before but still was unable to dance the Rumba.

He continued, "When you do the forward or backward step you pause or hold the step, ever so briefly and stiffen your leg, like so. When you start the count you step to your right side, quick, quick and then you bring your feet together. Hold. That's it, everything else you just keep saying those words—quick, quick, hold. Quick, quick, pause. Ready? Now let's try it."

Her chest pressed against his, her heart beat faster, her body was so close to his. Again her legs grew limp but she knew she could do this. She had to do this. She wanted so badly to do this. She took a deep breath, she did not want to leave his arms.

"Remember, start to your right side first," he said in his soothing voice, with the band playing distantly in the other room. "Quick, quick pause—quick, quick, hold. That's it, keep saying it your head, over and over."

She felt the rhythm, her body moving, brushing against his arms and his legs. The electricity between them was explosive and tingling, her body was doing some wonderful things to her. It was reacting in ways she had not experienced in years. He looked down at her and smiled. *Did he know what she was feeling?*

"Katherine, you are a natural dancer. Are you ready to try it on the dance floor? This carpet could twist your feet if we keep dancing here. Just remember to relax. As you pause for the hold step, if you like, for a real Cuban motion, you can sway your hips for that special effect, okay? Ready?"

"Oh, I don't know about that. I just know what you taught me here."

"Trust me?" he asked, with deep blue-grey eyes imploring her.

"Okay, but you'll… be… sorry!" she laughed.

"You'll do just fine."

She immediately felt at ease.

They made their way to the dance floor and she kept saying over and over again under her breath, "Quick, quick, hold—quick, quick, hold." The band leader waved a short salute which Jack returned in kind, smiling.

"You are doing fine," Jack told her as they danced the basic step again for a few moments before he separated from her and led her in a small turn away from him. "Just keep counting, that's all. Just keep counting." At the end of the turn she came back to him, smoothly, her breasts pressed firmly into his muscular chest. They danced around the dance floor to the tune of two more songs. She loved being held in his arms and as the music finally stopped playing she had no desire to let go.

"Yes, that was good," she smiled wanting more. "Can we do it again? she pleaded, now breathless." When the band finished she was so excited that she had finally learned the Rumba she thanked him and kissed him. She backed away, shocked at her own actions. "I'm sorry, I guess I got a little carried away."

His eyes were warm, inviting. "A beautiful woman should never have to apologize for kissing a man."

She smiled at his compliment. She never wanted this evening to end as she glanced at her watch, surprised at the late hour and knew she had to be up early for her move the next day.

"Jack, I hate to say this, but I have movers coming early in the morning and I am afraid I have to say good night." The band leader began to play *Gato Barberi's Europa* and waved at them. Jack smiled and waved goodnight after putting some money in the tip bowl.

"What was that all about?" Katie asked.

"He was playing an Argentine Tango. It is the sexiest dance that one can dance, very sensual. Most people only dance it with their spouses or lovers because you dance so very close, your body touching in so many ways, in so many places... if you know what I mean?"

She blushed imaging their bodies touching so close that she took his arm as he walked her back to the now deserted restaurant and waited with her while the valet got her car. She felt a slight tremble in her legs again and watched the traffic rush along beside them on the ocean highway.

"Maybe one day you will teach me the Argentine Tango?" she asked him.

"Perhaps, someday." He smiled, lost in her eyes.

"But I do want to wish you a Happy Birthday, Katie," he said, changing the subject. "I have had a great evening and hopefully I was an adequate substitute for your missing friend tonight."

"You were more than adequate, Jack. I had a great time. I did not want the evening to end."

"Nor did I. Would you like to join me for dinner tomorrow night when you get finished unpacking? Then you don't have to worry about cooking."

"Sure, I would like that, but I'm not sure what time I will be finished."

"That's fine. No rush. By the way, do you like fish?"

"I love fish. Especially fresh Pompano!"

"Well, whatever I catch tomorrow will be the catch of the day. Hopefully Pompano will be running tomorrow for you. Bring your appetite." He reached for his wallet and pulled out a business card. "Here's my card with my phone number and address. Just call me when you think you will be able to make it, so I can have everything ready. And if something comes up and you can't make it, I'll understand. And Katie, we are real casual at my beach place, all right?"

"Sure. I should be done with everything around five or six o'clock."

"Whenever you get done, come on over. I'm not real big on protocol as you can imagine. See you tomorrow?"

"I can't thank you enough," she said, while the valet pulled up behind them to deliver her car. She leaned up and kissed him on the cheek. "I'll see you tomorrow. Goodnight Jack."

He watched her car pull away, wishing he was going home with her tonight. He retrieved Duke from Tito telling him of his change in travel plans, then drove up the coast highway towards home, still enjoying the afterglow from his wonderful evening. The eviction notice glared at him from the front door when he arrived home, Ripping the bright yellow notice off the door, he said out loud to no one in particular, "Tomorrow we start to deal with these people."

Once inside the small bungalow, he noticed the tablets and empty wine glass sitting on the counter waiting for him. Its meaning seemed so long ago. He swept the no longer needed pills into the nearby trash container. "Time to go to bed, Duke. No more veal chops for you my friend. I am afraid you are stuck with me rather than Tito."

Two sets of eyes watched him through the window, cautiously, making unintelligible sounds which only they could hear and understand.

In Delray, some eight miles away, in the darkness of night, behind the building housing Katie's' secondhand bookstore, an equally set of ominous eyes watched Katie undress and slip into her night clothes.

"Just wait," said the low growl outside.

Chapter Nineteen

Senator Abe Swartzkopf was one of the most influential Senators on Capitol Hill. He'd been elected in eight landslide elections in New York and worked closely with the last six presidents. He knew how to come out on top and get his way, which he usually did.

"Senator," said his longtime aide, Margaret Thiess, briefing him on the day's upcoming busy schedule, "you have your meeting with the Senate Sub-Committee on Coastal Affairs at eleven o'clock. You have lunch with the President at the White House at one o'clock and the meeting with the full Ways and Means Committee at three o'clock." He nodded his agreement acting as if he was distracted but she knew he had a memory that never missed a detail, as a matter of fact, he never forgot anything.

Margaret continued, "This evening you are attending the presentation of the credentials from the new Ambassador from Brazil at the White House. The President will likely ask you to join them on the reception line because of your longtime acquaintance of their new official representative, Ambassador Joseph Morales."

The Senator listened to Meg reel off his calendar. She was always very thorough and very loyal and the Senator valued both of those admirable qualities.

"Senator, you are running three minutes behind schedule for a meeting with the bi-partisan committee on Intelligence and Criminal Affairs. If you hurry you can be there before the proceedings officially begin." He stood and removed his jacket hanging behind the door, slipping it over his shoulder.

"I will leave these messages on your desk for your attention when you return, Senator."

"Anything critical?" he asked. "No family emergencies, right? Family comes first, always."

"No Senator, but you did have one that I put near the top, I thought it would be of particular interest."

He picked up the pile of notes and messages and perused them until he saw a familiar name. He thumped his chest twice and told his assistant, "Call them and tell them I will be a few minutes late. Stall. I want to return this call."

She smiled. "Of course, Senator. I thought you would want to call him." She closed the door behind her and he picked up the phone to dial.

An alert voice answered on the other end. "Hello?"

"Hey Dr. Jack, how the hell are you?"

"Abe. Good to hear from you. How's the ticker?"

"Ever since you operated Doc and saved my life, it has been just fine. You know what they say, it takes a lickin' but keeps on tickin'." They both laughed.

"Keep the stress down Abe and it will last you even longer. Spend more time with the grandchildren and you'll live forever."

"I know, I know. I'll try, but you know how Washington is." He sat down in his large green leather chair, in his wood paneled office with pictures of his wife, four kids, and five grandkids prominently displayed on his desk. The only non-family picture he had on his desk was a picture of him and his wife Irene having dinner with Dr. Jack and his wife Laura. He lifted the photo and set it back down, slowly.

"What's up, Doc?"

"I need your help with something. I have a man down here in Florida that is pushing his weight around. Somehow he managed to have my house not only foreclosed on but also had an eviction notice posted on my front door. I have tried down here to get it squared away but they all seem to be connected in some way or another."

"What's this fellow's name?"

"His name is Scarlari, Victor Scarlari. Have you ever heard of him?"

"Can't say that I have Jack." He lied. "But give me some time and let me see what I can dig up, okay?"

"Sure, Abe. They are kicking me out of the house in two to three weeks. Anything you can do or direct me to someone who can, I would really appreciate it."

"Sure, Doc. Give me a little time and I'll get back to you."

Scarlari? Why did his name have to come up now of all times. The old Senator from New York leaned back in his chair and wrote down *Scarlari* on his note pad. He circled the name. Now he was stuck in the middle. What was he going to do? Abe Swartzkopf picked up the phone and dialed a familiar number. He would need to have this handled and handled very discretely.

Chapter Twenty

Igor Krushevnsky's limousine pulled in front of the New York skyscraper, one of many he owned along with his syndicate of other investors. His partner's names did not appear anywhere, on any documents, nor on any records but their word was their bond and they never broke their word. They were all part of the International Real Estate Cartel (IREC) and he was the recognized front man for the organization.

"Good morning, sir," said the bellman, opening the door for him.

"Yes, good morning," he grunted in response. His English was perfect having spent his university years at Oxford before going on to Harvard. He walked straight to the express elevator and was soon in his office on the fortieth floor, towering overhead and looking out over the city of New York below him.

"Give me the bad news first, always first," he said gruffly to Andre Pushkin, his chief of staff, who was never without his black leather notebook portfolio. Pushkin had been with him over six years but he never understood how Krushevnsky knew when there was a problem that needed to be dealt with immediately. He just seemed to have an innate six sense about such things.

"The property in Palm Beach did not close as expected and that will hold up our moving ahead with our project by at least thirty days, if not longer. Some doctor, a property owner, found a technicality in the auction documents and the local judge told our people they had to start over. We are looking at a lengthy delay."

"That is unacceptable," Igor shouted. "That is a four-hundred million dollar project! It is our first big one in Florida. I want to show our international investors that we can deliver and we are stopped by some local!" His face was bright red, the veins on his neck and forehead appeared they would burst at any moment. "Fix it! And fix it now," he screamed. "This property is crucial to IREC development! Do you hear me, Andre? Take care of it personally. Now get out and don't come back until it is fixed, do you understand?"

"Yes, sir," he responded and hustled out the door. His secretary Meloris appeared immediately after Andre's departure.

"Your vodka, sir, chilled, just the way you like it," she said. She came from the small Russian town of Borisovo just outside of Moscow. Krushevnsky only hired Russians. He felt they were the only ones he could trust and he paid them very well for that trust. But he could be ruthless to anyone who got in his way.

"Don't forget tonight, sir, you have the fundraiser to attend at seven for the U.S. Senate Political Action Committee (SPAC). You are their biggest contributor along with your friends, sir."

"Thank you Meloris." He watched her sexy body swaying from side to side as she walked away. She had a nice body, mused the big Russian, but she had never succumbed to his charms. Pity, she didn't know what she was missing. Pity.

He sipped his vodka and admired the view from his office. Another fundraiser tonight would make it easier for his empire to expand, just like in Florida. He needed that Palm Beach property and everything else would fall into place. He must have it! He was running out of time.

Chapter Twenty-One

Katie's movers were there right on time, showing up at exactly seven. She was ready and waiting. All week she had been moving things from one place to another over the past week in her SUV and now when she looked around she had very little left to move. By ten a.m. the movers had completed their job of moving all of her earthly belongings the short one mile distance to her new apartment. The only difference was here in her new place she owned the building.

She smiled as she started unpacking still thinking of her fairy tale dinner and evening with Jack. It was wonderful. But one thing still nagged her like an unreachable itch, she should have told him about the letters. She should have pushed it further.

Thinking about the letters she suddenly said out loud, "Where are the letters?" She began to panic. From her move everything was in an uproar and many items were misplaced. She searched frantically, inside all of her boxes, in the kitchen, the bedroom and they were nowhere to be found. Where were they?

She then noticed Felix sleeping on top of an old wine box and the blue papers sticking out from underneath her furry friend. She moved him out of harm's way and after depositing him on the sofa, sighed as she began to read another of his letters.

December, 2008

My Dearest Darling,

I felt a strong wind on my face today, the changing of the seasons I surmised. The wind and the sun reminded me of that free spirited summer when we took lessons to become sailors. The gusty wind and salty spray in our face. The instructor did not know what to make of us signing up to become certified sailors since most of the class participants were teenagers. The days in class and out on the boat with the boat reeling, then tacking were breathtaking. You handled it like an old salt. (I believe that is the term for a seasoned sailor.)

You sat tall, your eyes straight ahead then looked at me and whispered 'wonderful'. It was only then we noticed we were on a collision course with a huge oil tanker coming straight towards us. The instructor finally heeded my call for help and I could see the sweat pour from his face as he deftly maneuvered the sailboat out of harm's way, back to the pier. We laughed that night at dinner at what had happened. But remember how proud we were of our sailor pins? Your laugh, I remember when dancing, you would laugh sometimes for no reason as if someone unseen had told you, and only you, a joke.

I miss those times, my love. As I miss you. I miss your touch, your laugh, your smile your frown, I miss you. Remember this and remember me, my love. Always remember all of our memories, for that is what we have and that is what we cherish. I love you. Have to go.

Forever,

Jack.

Katie clutched the letter to her chest, suddenly feeling like an intruder—intruding on what Jack and his wife had together. What was she doing? Was she trying to pretend these letters were written to her? He would never forgive her if he knew she had the letters and did not tell him. She had met Jack and now felt worse reading the letters but she could not help herself.

She looked at the letters in her hand, staring at the firm scrolls and gentle loops of his elegant writing and decided she was going to return the letters, consequences be damned. She would give them back to him when the time was right. Besides, she had only a few more of the letters left to read, and then she would give them to him. All of them. But the letters brought her comfort and they were having a strange affect on her. She could not explain it. On the one hand she wanted to return the letters but on the other they were her security blanket. She never felt like this before and she could not explain it.

Katie finished unpacking and putting everything into its proper place and when she was done, she glanced at the large clock on the wall. It was two o'clock. She still liked the old time technology of clocks with hands on them. Most of the kids today viewed a watch or a clock as a novelty, preferring instead to rely on their cell phone for the time of day. She called the number on the card Jack gave her.

"Sorry, I'm not here. Leave me message at the beep. I'll phone you back. *BEEP!*"

"Jack it is two o'clock and I have some errands to run and then I will be over. Looking forward to it."

She remembered she promised to check on *Matey,* Jess's pet macaw. She would use the time now and go feed him at Jessie's store. She had tried to call Jessie in Chicago but got her voicemail. Driving down Third Avenue to Atlantic she parked the car behind the old yellow masonry building which housed Jessie's antique store.

Her cell phone rang and she reached for her purse beside her, it was Jessie calling.

"Hey Jess, how are you doing?"

"Not good, my aunt Sophia passed away last night right after I got here."

"Oh Jess, I am so sorry to hear that. We knew it was coming but it is still a shock when you finally hear it. You know you have my deepest condolences. Is there anything I can do to help?"

"No, just keep an eye on Matey for me."

"I just parked at your place now to feed him."

"Thanks Kate, I appreciate it."

"When are the services, Jess? I would like to fly out for them."

"Sophia is being cremated today and I am driving to the lake to spread the ashes there. She didn't leave much, mainly bills. But that is for another day. I already met with the estate attorney at the hospital, an old family friend and he is going to handle everything and just send me the papers to sign. I just wanted to let you know, maybe say some prayers if you would, okay?"

"Sure. I am so sorry. She was one of my favorites. I loved her sense of humor and her dry wit. She will be sorely missed."

"Thanks, Kate. I have to go. I need to talk to the funeral director. I just wanted to let you know what was going on. I'll see you soon. Good luck with the opening. Sorry I won't be there but I want you to have the best grand opening ever. You hear me? Ever! Take care and go get 'em!"

"Thanks Jess, I love you."

"Love ya too. See ya soon."

The death put a damper on the Katie but she was determined to move forward. Losing a close loved one like Sophia was the worst thing that could happen and she felt sorry for Jessie and was going to miss her at her grand opening tomorrow.

Jessie's store was closed, since Jessie had no one else working for her. Her aunt had been ill off and on for the last two years and she was constantly closing the store to rush to Chicago to tend to her. Katie knew that Jess was also sending her money to help her aunt out financially, although Katie felt Jess could not really afford to do so.

It seemed so different in the antique shop with the lights out and not hearing Jessie's laughter circulating through the shop. The air was stale and had a slight musty smell. Jess said that is the smell her clients liked and paid high prices for all her "finds." To Katie it was just old stuff.

She went inside, towards the rear of the store and immediately heard Matey holler out in a booming voice, "Welcome, Welcome." Katie had taken care of Matey many times before and she knew the routine.

"How ya doin', Matey?"

"Matey is good. Welcome."

Katie went into Jess's office, turned on the light and pulled Matey's food tray from the fridge. She filled his feeder and as she closed the fridge some papers blew off Jess's desk. Katie bent over and picked it up and laid the note back on Jessie's desk, shocked to see it was an eviction notice. Other bills were stacked high on her desk, all marked past due in large stamped red letters.

Jess was always so positive and so supportive of all of Katie's efforts, she never dreamed Jess was having so many problems. She felt so self-centered not seeing the problems before. She gently set the bills back down on her desk and left to feed Matey.

She was disturbed by what she'd seen. Jessie never once mentioned she was having financial problems. But Katie never thought to ask, to really understand what was going on in her life. She was more concerned about moving on with her own life after her divorce from Richard than trying to help Jessie. Jessie was a good businesswoman and very astute. She would need to talk with her when she returned from Chicago.

• • • • •

Katie turned onto I-95 and headed South towards Boca Raton, only ten minutes past Jess's store. She pulled off onto Glades Road and parked the car on the Mega-booksellers lot. She had finished reading one of the poetry books, by Allison White which had been mixed in with the romance novels she bought from Jack and she fell in love with the poet's writings. The writer was a wonderful poet. So vibrant, so touching and real. Katie wanted more books by her. She approached the customer service counter and asked the white haired lady behind the desk for help.

"I am looking for any poetry books you may have by Allison White."

"Oh yes, right this way, follow me to the poetry section. White was very good," said the woman. She checked the shelf, then kneeling her knees made a unique popping sound. "It's a bitch getting old," she cracked and began checked again. "Here it is, I have her latest one titled, *Yearnings*. Unfortunately it is her last one."

"Her last one?"

"Yes, she died just a while back. She was very much a romantic but very, very good. You feel you are listening in on someone's intimate conversation. Do you like Elizabeth Barrett Browning or Robert Frost?"

"Yes, I love them."

"If you like them you will also like this book by Allison White. Enjoy."

"Thank you," Katie said, paging randomly through the book, deciding whether or not to buy it.

She stopped in the middle of the aisle, reading, overcome by emotions pouring from her newly discovered author,

Oh thy shallow mind doest creep—Into my heart of dreams so wonderfully deep—
For you my love to sort and tarry through the fog seen moors,
Take my soul and hold my heart's desire.
Quench my thirst by sunrise and hold me forever time, yes time my love, time.
Yet take haste in thy dark abode—Where thy power reach my tethered soul
Oh my heart yearns for thee—mine timbered eyes crash across the sea
Urgently pulsing for you, for you my love, to hark, to hear, and to hold...

Whew! Yes, I want this book! She continued to read while advancing to the checkout counter. This lady can write poetry, she thought to herself. She could feel her pain and desire, as it oozed passion from the pages of her mind.

She read more of the book in the car and realized why she loved poetry so much, it was what you made of it that made it so powerful.

She glanced at her watch and headed for the address listed on Jack's card. Tonight she was on her way to have dinner with Jack! But she was also worried about how Jess was holding up.

The drive to his place seemed to take forever. She turned North on A1A at the end of Ocean Avenue and after driving along the coast highway she realized she may have passed his house. She turned around and drove slowly back in the direction she had just come.

Katie could not see many of the homes along the road, most were hidden by oversized landscaping. She looked up ahead and saw the roof of a small cottage off to the left high above the ocean. It was surrounded by sand dunes filled with shrubs and overgrown mahogany trees and wild Sea Grape plantings buffering each side. She slowed and checked the address from Jack's business card before turning into the driveway.

The loose gravel made a crushing noise as she applied the brakes and brought her SUV to a sudden halt. She grabbed the bottle of wine from the seat beside her and walked towards the house. The house was up a small hill, with sand dunes on both sides protecting it from the elements and hiding it from view.

Katie tread up a set of wooden steps, embedded in the side of the earthen hill around the side of the house. The bushes on the pathway had been recently trimmed and the house sported a fresh coat of brown paint making it feel so very comfortable, drawing her closer inside. The shutters on the windows made the cottage feel more like a home on Cape Cod than a beach house on the Treasure Coast in Palm Beach. Yes, this was Jack's home, she could feel him in everything she saw.

There were two large panels at the top of the garage door and she could see a car inside the garage. It must be Jack's car, it was a tan, four door Mercedes. It was as if she had just seen an affirmation she was getting closer to seeing him again. Her heart paced faster at the thought of it.

She made her way up the steps to the front door. There was a small covered wooden roof protecting the porch which contained two large sea foam green Adirondack chairs, set side by side with a small wooden table between them. She knocked on the front door, then turned to look around. The broad ocean crashed hard, waves rolled in and out, sending large plumes of white water high into the air. She knocked again. Still no response.

Just then a loud bark came from the beach. Duke ran towards her at full speed and when he reached her, nearly knocked her over. He was all over her with kisses, licking and slobbering. He was slobber machine. Then she saw Jack.

He stood on the beach casting a large surf fishing rod far out into the waves. He had another rod stuck into a rod holster anchored securely into the sand. He had fish strike, and was trying to reel it in. It was fighting back, causing Jack to strain in his surf harness, his muscles pulled tight, trying to outwit or outfight his opponent. The huge fish finally gave up and succumbed to fate. He began to reel him in.

"Hi," she said, "What did you catch?"

He smiled without taking his eyes off of his catch.

"Dinner," he responded, not the least bit startled to see her. "It rained here until just a half an hour ago. I know you said you loved Pompano. So you will get your wish. They haven't been biting at all until now. I told myself that if I didn't catch anything by now, I would just go to Publix's and buy whatever they had fresh. But it tastes so much better when it is as fresh as this."

He reeled the silver and yellow fish in while she admired his tanned, well-defined muscles coursing up and down his arms. His chest was flat like a washboard. She could easily count his abdominal muscles and found herself filling with desire.

His shirt was off and she could not help but notice he had a number of large black and brown scars across his broad back and muscular shoulders. The scars were deep and looked recent.

"Ready?" he asked, distracting her when he noticed her looking at his back. He quickly grabbed his chambray shirt from the nearby beach chair and threw it on, then smiled, while holding the Pompano high for her to admire. They grabbed up everything from the beach and headed back towards the little beach house just as it started to rain.

"Sorry I was not there at the house to greet you when you got here, I thought you would probably be later. But I did so want to give you the Pompano you like."

"No problem. I got finished early today."

"I tell you what, let me clean the fish, take a shower and I will be ready and presentable in twenty minutes tops. In the meantime, if you don't mind, you can grab the wine from the fridge, open it and pour us each a glass."

"Sounds like a plan, Jack." She loved saying his name, having read his signature so many times in his letters. Yes, he would always be, *Forever Jack*.

She opened the wine, poured two glasses and then placed the bottle into an ice bucket to keep it chilled. Katie walked around the living room holding her wine, looking at the few items Jack had posted on the wall. He had his University degree from Duke University and his medical degree from Harvard posted side by side. There was also framed letter of appreciation from an organization called DIW. Katie was not familiar with the group.

She looked at the pictures on the small end table. They appeared to be pictures of his son's family, including the grandkids. She stopped and lifted a picture of him with his arms around another woman.

"That was Laura, my wife," Jack said walking up behind her, tucking in his shirt. "I lost her two years ago, to pneumonia."

Katie could feel the heat emanating from his body, he was so close. His aftershave scent was enticing but only just barely noticeable. It was intoxicating.

"She was very beautiful," Katie said.

"Yes, she was. It is hard to think of her in the past tense. I still feel she is all around me like she never left. She was fun to be with and would try anything. She had a great sense of humor and in some ways…, you remind me of her."

Katie turned to look at him as he returned the picture to the small table. His pain was still very visible. She wanted to reach out to him, to comfort him, to hold him, but she dare not lest she chase him away.

"Dinner is almost ready," he said, almost in a whisper, and then he headed for the kitchen.

She followed him in and helped to prepare, handing him his glass of wine. "Here's to dinner." They toasted their glasses.

The meal was like having her own private gourmet chef. He was a fantastic cook, starting first with an arugula salad, with fresh mushrooms, onions, bacon bits and Jack's homemade dressing. The fish was sautéed to perfection, with the slivered almond asparagus topping it was out of this world. For dessert he made a wonderful chocolate lava cake, which had streams of chocolate sliding down the sides and it melted in her mouth. She had never tasted a meal so good.

She sat on the porch, relegated there by Jack, as he cleaned the table and the kitchen. He soon appeared with a small glass of homemade Limoncello.

"You know this is the secret ingredient that Café Luna use's on their baked garlic. They use it to take away the harshness of the garlic."

"You don't say," Jack responded, as they sat on the two porch chairs, watching the lightning storms dance upon the horizon in the distance. "How do you know that?"

"Tito told me," she said, her eyes wide in a triumphant gaze.

"You know I have been going there for years and have always asked him what they used but he would never tell me. 'Family Secret' is all he would say to me. But what do you know? Limoncello, of course that makes sense. I am amazed you got it out of him. He would not even tell that secret to Laura and she was one of his favorites."

"I must have the magic touch," smiled Katie. They sat and were mesmerized by the rise and fall of the ocean waves, crashing on the beach, just enjoying each other's company.

"Jack, I noticed a letter on the wall from an organization I was unfamiliar with, DIW or something along those lines. What is that?"

"I used to work for them for a long time until recently. It stands for Doctors International Worldwide. As a matter fact, Laura was a nurse for them and we would many times travel together."

"What do they do?"

"We would travel worldwide administering shots, performing exams, setting up health care clinics around the globe. We also went into refugee camps in an effort to reduce malaria and diphtheria, smallpox and other diseases that spread so rapidly in camps like those. It was one of the most fulfilling experiences I have ever had. We sometimes would be asked to go into war zones to treat the locals who got caught up in the crosshairs of the fighting."

She looked at him with such great respect.

"Hey," he said when he noticed her admiring goo-goo eyes, "It was just a job, just like all of the other jobs."

"Yeah, sure, Jack," she joked. "Well, as much as I hate to go, I really must be on my way," she said, lifting herself from the chair on the porch, with the pounding surf coming closer up the beach. She always seemed to be saying those words to him but only she knew how much she wanted to stay with him.

He walked her to her car and opened the car door. "Tomorrow is my big day," she explained. "My grand opening. You are coming, aren't you?"

"Yes, of course I am coming. I will definitely be there."

She looked him in the eyes and their gazes fixed on one another.

He kissed her the forehead and then softly on the cheek. He pulled her close. Electricity jolted through her body as their lips met. She quivered under his touch. He pulled her closer, until she could feel his heart pounding against her breasts. She never wanted this kiss to end. She didn't want to leave, even though she had to. She wanted *him*, now.

"Goodnight," he said, stepping back.

"Goodnight," she said, pausing to take a deep gasp of air.

She started to turn around, when he said again, "Goodnight Katie, I will see you tomorrow." His hand lingered on her shoulder. She drove away, heading home, still warm from his touch and embrace. She could not wait until tomorrow.

Jack watched her drive away, the tail lights from her car disappearing down the road. He watched even though he could no longer see her, frozen in time recalling words from his past.

"Life is making a commitment," he remembered Laura was fond of saying. "Dead people do not have that luxury." The night air carried the scent of the wild beach flowers swirling around the house.

When he turned around he saw them, two huge men, dressed in black, pistols stuck in their belts. The bigger one shoved a revolver against his stomach. "Turnaround Doc, we are going for a ride, lover boy."

The thug shoved Jack backward using the gun at his midsection. The other one, ordered him with one simple word, "Move." A large black sedan pulled in front of the beach house and they wedged Jack between them in the rear seat. Silence filled the air and accompanied them on their journey. *Who are these guys? Where were they taking him?*

• • • • •

Katie undressed, wondering what tomorrow would bring. She could only dream. She missed Jack already, she could still feel his strong arms around her and she decided this time, she was not going to fight it. She was not going to reason it away. She was just going to follow her heart. She painted with her eyes open and could see wonderful and mysterious things unfolding as she was swept away to sleep.

The man with dark watching eyes stepped from the shadows and made his way to the rear door. It was locked when he tried to open it. He would not be denied his prize again, he pulled a large piece of metal blind from inside his jacket and wedged it inside the door until it sprang open. He was finally inside.

He made his way into the dark, not needing any light, walking up the steps towards her bedroom. It was quiet as he turned the bedroom doorknob. "Now," he commanded, "now Katie will be mine! Yes!"

His watching and waiting were over. He shoved the bedroom door open wide and turned on the light. The room was empty! She had moved! His hellfire scream traveled down the dark steps to journey outside and mingle with the noise of the rustling leaves. Again and again he screamed in pain. "NO! NO! NO!" He would not be denied. He would find her. And then he would have her!

Chapter Twenty-Two

The car rambled down the now deserted streets of West Palm Beach, past the houses all lined in a row until the sedan reached the rundown abandoned industrial areas by the docks. Jack did not recognize any landmarks, as they drove past one nondescript industrial building after another.

He was wedged between two big goons and the rear of the car was quickly filled with the competing stench of putrid body odor and stale after shave, coupled with the overwhelming smell of vodka. Jack was beginning to gag from the overwhelming odors.

"Can you open a window, please?" he pleaded with his captors. "I desperately need some fresh air."

"*Nyet*," responded the big one to his right.

After passing the third low steel windowless building, the silent driver made a sharp left, then a right and before finally stopping in front of a pier building where two other cars were parked, waiting. Waiting for him.

When the car pulled to an abrupt stop, the big thug sitting to his left, the one they called Ivan, grabbed him by the shirt and yanked him from the car, throwing him towards the waiting limousine. Standing beside the long sedan were three men.

The big goons shoved Jack towards the waiting group. A tall well dressed man approached him.

"Good evening, Dr. Petersen. How are you? Walk with me, will you please?" His perfectly tailored European suit stood in stark contrast to Jack's casual beach wear from his evening spent with Katie. He walked barefoot with this new stranger, with Jack detecting a slight Russian accent.

"Russian?" Jack asked.

"Very good," he replied, "but no, I am from the Ukraine."

They walked along the deserted pier, alone, looking out over the industrial canals that lined the pier with piles of trash floating by undisturbed. His two body guards walked behind them.

"Do you know there are more dead bodies and unsolved murders from this pier than from any other area in South Florida?"

"No, I didn't know that," Jack responded, stepping around piles of broken glass, which littered the area.

"Yes, that is a fact. There are more murders here than in the drug areas of Moscow or New York and you know what? Nobody seems to care." He stopped and turned to face Jack. The doctor could see his face clearly now, the flickering streetlight glimmered shards of light onto his once partially hidden face.

"Dr. Petersen, I will make this very simple for you." He reached inside his jacket and Jack instinctively stepped backwards, expecting another gun to appear. The well spoken Ukrainian instead brought out a document and handed it to him.

"My employer has bought your property from an auction as one piece to a very large puzzle, a redevelopment plan here in South Florida. He bought it fairly, using your system here in the United States. But now, you are the only thing standing in his way. He is not happy. Here is my proposal…, sign this bill of sale and you drive away tonight, a free man."

"Or?" Jack asked.

"Or the newspapers will report, buried on page forty-three of tomorrow's edition, that a man's body was found dead with a bullet hole into his head. He was found floating in the canal in the pier district. His disabled car was found nearby. The police have no suspects in the case and foul play is suspected." He smiled when he finished his proposed news report. "The police won't even investigate your death, Dr. Petersen. We brought your car right outside the industrial park here. It is up to you if you drive away tonight or if the police find it tomorrow morning with the wires disabled. It is up to you." The Ukrainian proffered a pen to Jack.

"I don't really have much of a choice, do I?"

"No you don't, Dr. Petersen. And the police will be of little help because if you go to them the result will remain the same," he said, gesturing toward the murky water in the canal.

He took the pen and signed the document, while asking him, "You work for Scarlari?"

The tall Ukrainian laughed out loud, visibly amused. "Scarlari? Scarlari is a pussy cat compared to my boss. No, Dr. Petersen, I do not work for Scarlari. You will find your car at the end of this pier, off to the left. It was a pleasure meeting you, even under these terrible circumstances. Goodnight." He handed Jack the familiar key ring with his Mercedes keys attached.

Jack carefully walked towards his car, picking his way through the glass piles. He watched the convoy of waiting vehicles pull away, leaving a bewildered Jack standing in the still night air. What had just happened?

Chapter Twenty-Three

Today is my day, Katie thought, stretching her arms wide to greet and embrace a new chapter in her life. *What was the old phrase? Today is the first day of the rest of your life. Sounds corny, but true.*

Although she had held out little hope, she'd found Jack and if she didn't screw it up like she screwed up everything else, it may go somewhere. But today was the Grand Opening of her new gallery, something she had not done in many, many years. Katie was nervous, lying in bed thinking of everything that could go wrong.

"Too late now," she confided to her still asleep feline friend, Felix. "The die is cast. Let's get a move on."

She had tried to reach Jessie three times and texted her twice but was unable to reach her. She would try again after breakfast but the silence from her good friend was deafening. *Not good*, she thought, dressing for the new day.

Katie went downstairs and made one final check of the gallery, everything seemed to be in order. Now she was getting excited. By four p.m., when the caterers arrived, she knew she was well on her way. She returned upstairs to dress for the evening. Jack would be there tonight, she thought, she wanted to show him her art work and gain his opinion. She missed him already. She smiled at the thought of him and her wonderful evening last night. It had been magical.

She reached for the comfort of one of his letters, one of his last letters, she had only a few more left to read. Then she knew she would have to return them but for now, she began to read.

February, 2009

My Dearest Darling,

It rained today. Saying that it rained is an understatement, it actually poured. Remember the time when we arrived in London and it rained for three days straight but we still enjoyed it? Our favorite city delivered up its secrets that week, since we focused on places to go that would keep us dry.

Remember the afternoon at the Sherlock Holmes Pub? While we were having a pint of beer and a bit of lunch, a nearby group of women were getting "toasted" at the English version of a bridal shower. They called it a "hen party." They began a conga line through the whole bar and making their way out into the wet street and back again out of the pouring rain. They grabbed your arm to join them and, where you go I follow. Soon we were all dancing on the small dance floor inside the pub. A wonderful day! Remember?

The part of the trip I remember most fondly, was our visit to the British Museum. What a place! Remember, the day we were looking for the Rosetta Stone, from Egypt? We looked everywhere and we both thought it was a small stone. Boy were we wrong. It was the size of two cinder blocks.

Do you recall walking through the Egyptian "mummy" exhibit? Seeing the Elgin Marbles? Marveling at the gold of Tutankhamen? Of all the times we have been to London, that was my most favorite trip. We would walk, hand in hand, your hand tightly clutching mine, while sometimes you would rub it across your cheek. It was on that trip you told me you were pregnant. We were both so happy.

I love you and I love saying those magical words to you. I only wish I were there to see the smile on your face when I said the words. I love you, always remember that. Must go now.

Forever,

Jack

Katie folded the letter and breathed a deep sigh, holding it close. Though she found the letters comforting in their own way, the letters now were no substitute for holding Jack in her arms. But they still reminded her of the romance left within his heart.

She had hoped to have Jessie there for her grand opening for moral support but it looked like it was not to be. The evening was going to be a long one based upon her many past grand openings in New York, she dressed for the special evening in a soft colored silk blouse with a pair of beige linen pants, her new choice of comfort for the summer. After a quick brush and a flip of the hair, a dab of makeup, after an hour, Katie looked in the mirror, she was ready.

The downstairs where the catering company was setting up needed her attention as the tuxedoed waiters gathered their trays and the violinist sampled the hors d'oeuvres.

Katie stood in the middle of the room and said to those getting ready for the evening's festivities, " Hello! Hello! Can I have your attention, please. I want to thank all of you here tonight because without you this party cannot be a success. I ask you to please treat this event as a welcome home party, as if those here tonight are your closest friends." The room became silent, listening to her.

"The people coming here tonight are very important but I want them, and I want all of you, to have a wonderful time. Relax, enjoy the art, have some hors d'oeuvres, listen to the music, mingle with the guests and help me make my customers feel as welcome here as you would want your friends to feel welcome in your own home." The whole room broke out in applause. Katie was a good person to work for, she was caring, honest, fair and giving, what more could you ask for in an employer?

"Let the party begin," she said with a smile and unlocked the front door. The music began playing and customers were soon strolling inside and by six o'clock the newest gallery in Delray Beach was filled with people. It was going so well.

She noticed the art critics from two of the largest regional newspapers walking slowly around the gallery and taking notes and one from the TV station KTFL setting up cameras for an interview with Katie. The reviews she heard while walking around were all gushing with compliments and all favorable.

Then she saw Jess walk hurriedly through the gallery. Katie's face beamed. She went to her and gave her a hug.

"I am so sorry about your Aunt Sophia," Kate whispered. "And I am glad you made it."

"Thanks but I wouldn't miss it for the world. Get me a drink there girl and let this shindig begin. Nice crowd, I could use a crowd like this in my shop."

They toasted each other with a glass of champagne. Katie could tell something else was bothering her best friend.

"What's wrong, Jess?"

Jess got serious. "I was going to tell you later so as not to spoil your special day but Katie I am closing the shop next week. I been away from the business for too long in order to help out with my aunt and my business has suffered. Customers never knew when I would be open or when I would be closed."

Katie took Jess aside saying quietly, "Jess you know, this whole gallery venture is proving to be more than I am going to be able to handle. What with my painting, the school and running the Gallery and making time to see Jack, I just don't know if I can do it all? My new art training school is oversubscribed. What about you coming here to work for me and running the business side of the gallery? What do you say?"

"Who's Jack? Is that the Jack I think it is? When did all of this happen? I was only gone for a couple of days," she said, oblivious to everything else Katie had said.

"He will be here later tonight, I hope," her voice full of enthusiasm. "I'll fill you in later. What do you say?"

"I didn't want to spoil your Grand Opening and all, but I think it is time to shut down the shop, so why not? Yes, I accept your offer. We can talk about everything else tomorrow. You found Jack?"

"Yes, I can't wait to tell you all about it. I met him at…"

Katie's attention was diverted by a large commotion at the front door due to a sudden flurry of activity. She could not see what the commotion was about. An increasing buzz followed a small group of people around the side of the gallery, up the small aisle until standing right in front of Kate, was the diminutive, grey-haired but feared *Times of New York* Art Critic, Sara Klein Reinhardt.

Dressed in a Coco Chanel outfit and sporting the latest Jimmy Choo shoes, she was known to make or break a gallery with the first words of her review. The wealthy of New York came in droves to build huge estates in the warm climate of South Florida and with them came their decorators and architects. The market to them was immense but one discouraging word from Sara could sink Katie's newest endeavor.

She slowly approached Katie, with a scowl on her face and stood directly in front of her. The music stopped playing, the waiters were motionless as her eyes narrowed on Katie. Then she gave the assembled art loving crowd what they were all waiting to hear, her verdict.

Sara grabbed Katie— who gazed at her with terror—by her shoulders. "Kate, my dear… Fabulous, simply fabulous!" The crowd applauded and the music began again as Katie let out a sigh of relief.

She brushed a kiss, kiss, on each of Katie's cheeks and whispered close in her ear, "It is so good to have you back on the art scene. We will make this gallery bigger than ever before. Come on, let's show them what we have for them back in New York." She motioned to the camera crew who set up a remote feed back to the New York TV station KTNY and she held up a microphone.

"Good evening, ladies and gentlemen. This is Sara Klein Reinhardt and I am here reporting from the sunny South Florida city of Delray Beach. We are here tonight to celebrate a rebirth, a renaissance, a showering of welcome rain on this parched world of art, with the opening of the newest, and finest art gallery in South Florida, *Katherine's*. I am with a familiar face to those who remember the golden age of art galleries, Katherine Kosgrove. It has been a long time Katherine. It is so good to see you back in the art business. Your talents and keen eye have been sorely missed."

"Thank you, Sara. It is good to be back. I have missed the art world but I am back now."

"Well, it is good to have you back. Let me ask you Katherine…"

Katie's gaze saw Jack as he walked in the front door. He smiled at her and picked up a glass of champagne from one of the roving waiters. Her heart soared.

"So what do you think, Katherine? Will this gallery be a success? Will you succeed where so many others have failed?" Sara asked with a knowing smile as to the answer.

Jack walked toward her. *Focus on the interview.* He held a red rose in his hand and was walking closer towards her pretending to inspect the art on the walls.

"Katherine? What do you think?" asked Sara, with a pursed smile on her lips.

"Sara, with help from people like yourself, who appreciate fine art, this gallery will succeed and flourish."

Jack stood looking at her favorite painting, one inspired by his letters. *How appropriate.*

Sara's interview rambled on about the nature of the art at the new gallery and the new art school that Katherine had set up but her words were more like the murmur of a bee, droning on and on.

Finally she heard, "This is Sara Klein Reinhardt signing off from Delray Beach Florida at the home of the newest grand art gallery, *Katherine's.*"

The bright television lights were shut off and soon the gallery resumed its pulse of activity. Katie searched the room for Jack and saw him once again looking at her, smiling. He waved. She made her way to him, nearly running. She could see him just beyond the edge of the crowd. Just a minute more, there he is she thought, she felt like a giddy school girl again. She laughed at herself as she rushed towards him.

The space in front of her was suddenly filled by the presence of a large suit jacket blocking her way and her view of Jack. She stepped to her right and then to her left and the jacket was still there. She looked up to see who the suit jacket belonged to. Why was he blocking her way?

It was Richard…, her ex-husband.

Chapter Twenty-Four

"Katie girl! How the hell are you?" Richard said, picking her up off the ground and spinning her around, kissing her and hugging her.

Irritation and shock collided. "Richard? Put me down!"

He finally set her back on the ground, pulling her close, holding her hostage and kissing her hard on the lips as she struggled to get from his clutches.

"What the hell are you doing here?" She pushed him away, took a step back and glared at him.

"Well the firm is opening a new office here in South Florida and guess who they chose to come down here and spearhead the opening?" He spread his arms wide. "Yours truly."

Katie narrowed her eyes. "What do you mean?"

"My firm has finally decided to expand and one of the areas they see great potential in is here in South Florida. I have been pushing them for the past couple of months and they finally have agreed with me. Isn't it great? We can get back together again, Kate." He stepped forward to hug her again. She pushed him away.

"Richard you left me for some twenty-something tart. She was old enough to only remember two presidents. And you want me to take you back? What happened? She kicked you out didn't she? I knew it."

"Hello Richard," said Jessie pushing her way through the gawking crowd. "Maybe we need to move from here and take this discussion to the other room?" Jessie joined in the fray and ushered them away from the crowded room. "We don't need to have the whole world knowing our business now do we?"

"Yes, good idea," said Richard.

But Katie had other ideas. She didn't want to have a private discussion with the man who'd ruined her life. She wanted him gone. She stopped and met Richard's gaze. "Richard I want you to leave and leave now." She spun around and headed back towards where she had last seen Jack. When she reached the front of the store, she found an abandoned red rose lying on a table. Katie glanced in the other room of the gallery but Jack was nowhere to be seen. She picked up and smelled the delicious flower before reading the attached note.

Katie-
Good luck in your new venture.
One day, I would love to teach you the Argentine Tango.
Jack

She held the note in her hand, looking at the beautiful scrolls of his handwriting, these letters she would know anywhere. A tear dripped down onto the fragile flower. This was supposed to be a happy day for her but Richard had ruined it. Jack was gone again, nowhere to be seen. Her shoulders slumped. Richard stood with a group of people, drinking champagne and nibbling on the trays of food the waiters were bringing around. It was all his fault. When he saw her looking at him he raised his champagne glass in a toast that she could not hear. She would just have to ignore him—luckily he didn't stick around long.

In the end, the grand opening was a huge success. Katie had sold over ten paintings and had commissions for six more. She had piles of business cards of decorators wanting her to begin special paintings for their clients. She was happy but at the same time sad, when she plopped into her chair watching the caterers clear out the last of the tables.

Jessie joined her in the back office, handing her a glass of champagne. "Here's to you, Kate. You did real good, boss."

"I don't feel like I did good. Yes, the gallery opening tonight was a success but I wanted everything to be perfect. Then Richard shows up and spoils everything, as usual. I could never count on him to do anything except screw things up." Katie sat there dejected lost in her thoughts, withdrawing into herself.

"The night we were supposed to have dinner and Sophia took ill, well Jack showed up."

"Jack? Jack the handsome beast from the flea market? That Jack?"

"Yes. And we hit it off pretty good. I invited him to the opening and then Richard shows up and screws up everything. Damn him. I really like this guy Jack and so would you. We seemed to mesh and now…"

"Don't just sit there feeling sorry for yourself. Kate, go get him if he means that much to you. Fight for him. Go! I'll finish up here. Just go. Tell him how you feel. Put it out there, you won't help yourself sitting here. Go find out if it is for real or not. Find out now. Don't regret it later, believe me. Go!"

"You're right, Jess."

The moon shone its bright gold glow over the sea as Katie drove down the ocean highway towards Jack's house. She pulled into his driveway and walked up the wide wooden steps to the front door. Owls hooted in the evening moon glow. She knocked. She could hear the ocean waves crashing on the beach behind her, so melodic and so rhythmic, so intoxicating.

She glanced at the chairs on the porch and then she saw him, sitting in the moonlight. He must have been sleeping because he startled and gazed over at her. "Kate? Is that you?" He stood to face her.

"Yes," she said taking his hand.

He breathed deep before saying, "I'm sorry I had to leave so suddenly but something came up."

"I understand, Jack. The man you saw tonight was Richard, my ex-husband."

"Kate you don't owe me an explanation, you don't owe me anything." He started to turn away.

She touched his arm. "Jack, I want to explain. It is important to me that you understand. That man you saw tonight was my ex-husband. I did not invite him to the gallery." She stopped for a minute and took in a deep breath. "I did not even know he was in town. He just showed up but I am glad now that he did. You see, I thought I still had feelings for him until I saw him tonight and realized I was wrong. It is over between him and I. You see, I don't have feelings for him but I do feel drawn to you. I find myself wanting to be with you more than anyone else."

"Kate, I have strong feelings for you but I don't want to complicate your life or mine if there is already someone else. I'm glad to hear it is over between the two of you. I would never want to hurt you or cause you any pain." He took her hand as the sound of the ocean waves crashed on shore and the moonlight glistened off the waves. His hand sent shivers through her, the words would not come, her emotions were building. *Say something, anything!*

"Jack, I bought a book of poetry yesterday," she gulped, almost stuttering trying to regain her composure. "It is a book written by Allison White. I found a poem in the book which describes my feeling so much better than I could ever express them. Let me see if I

can remember the words, bear with me. Oh yes, I remember now."
She faced him.

"Bring light those memories weep - life in past will never be
sweet kiss do I give thee - longing desires leap forth, yearning only for thee
Oh thy mystery well, so deep - bring my hearts with secrets keep
That was my past for evermore
list not those dark shadows but bring forth light to soar
Forgive my soul to forget the past - Love, my love is only meant to last
Kiss my lips forever sealed, take my heart unto your hands
My soul, my heart are yours for thine to command..."

"Jack," she breathed deep, looking at him while holding his hands in hers. "I would like you to teach me the Argentine Tango, teach me the dance of love, show me, guide me, lead me, I am yours," Katie breathed the whisper into his ear, then gazed again deep into his eyes.

Jack took her into his arms, drawing her close, closer than she had ever been held by him before. She surrendered herself to him. Went to him without conditions, as the kiss she had been waiting for, found its way to her lips.

Katie's heart leaped, pulsing hard. Her legs quivered in wanting desire. Her palms and the treasure between her thighs were moist, while her skin tingled. She was losing control as she kissed him.

Their kiss deepened. Bending down, he lifted her into his arms and carried her upstairs to his bedroom, before gently depositing her on the bed.

"Katherine, let me teach you the dance of love. The dance of lovers and forever soul mates."

She touched him, yearned for him, as she pulled him onto the bed to join her.

The waves crashed hard outside the cabin. The pounding and relentless surf pushing the sea to its ebb and flow. Strong waves rushing then retreating in their endless cycle. The moon shone brightly on the beach reflecting on the waves like a shadow. The night settled in their arms like lovers found.

Outside on the dunes, two sets of vigilant eyes watched the small beach cottage, observing. Nothing escaped their gaze.

Chapter Twenty-Five

The sun peeked through the front upstairs bedroom window which overlooked the ocean as the golden orb began to rise over the horizon of waves. Katie could feel Jake's chest rise and fall beneath her palm. Soft light picked up the slight reddish hue of his chest hairs, reflecting his Irish descent. She brushed his chest softly with her hand and twirled the hairs around her finger.

He breathed in deep saying, "Good morning. Sleep well?"

"Yes." She shifted closer to him. "I slept very well." She reached for his hand and intertwined her fingers with his, her leg draped over his, feeling his warmth all over her body. He leaned over and kissed her, holding her in his arms. "You dance very, very well, my dear."

"You are not so bad either."

"How about some breakfast?" he asked as they could both smell the wonderful aroma of freshly brewed coffee making its way up the steps to the bedroom.

"I would love some breakfast."

He kissed her lips and turned to stand, revealing the large scars on his back.

"Jack? Whatever happened to your back?" She touched the deep scars softly. "You have scars all over it."

He froze but did not turn around. "I worked at my uncle's lumber yard working my way through school and I backed into the branding machine."

"But these scars look more recent. I think they look…"

"Cream and sugar in your coffee?" he asked, changing the subject.

"Yes, thank you. I'll be right down."

She watched him stand, get dressed with his fine physique framed by the window. Desire flowed through her, again. He sounded evasive about the scars but she decided not to bring them up again.

Katie dressed and joined him downstairs. She found him in the kitchen, and walking past began running her hand across his shoulder, then kissed his neck.

"Ham and eggs okay, with some toast and marmalade?" he asked, handing her a mug of coffee.

"You read my mind." The morning sunrise began its daily journey into the sky in all of its glory out over the ocean.

"That poem you recited to me last night, where did you find it?"

"I bought it from you at the flea market. It was a book of poetry by Allison White. I loved it so much I went to Book Universe Mega-Books and bought another one called *Yearnings*. I love poetry in general but I really love her poetry. It was so appropriate for last night."

"Yes, I love her as well," he told her.

She looked at him astonished, he was always surprising her. A man that loved and appreciated poetry was a different species entirely.

"Breakfast is ready!" he proclaimed. "If you can grab the coffee mugs, we can eat outside if you like?"

"Wonderful!"

The ocean air breeze was refreshing as they made their way to the outside porch. A small casserole dish lay on the welcome mat by his front door. Setting down breakfast on the wooden side table outside, he picked up the casserole dish and looked at the note which was taped to it.

Jack unfolded the note and began to read out loud, "*Jack, enjoy the pasta! Missed seeing you around. See you soon. Toodles, Ginny.*"

"Ah ha! I'm not the only one who has a secret admirer pop up," Katie said. "Who's Ginny?"

"She was a friend in the neighborhood where I used to live. Part of the reason I moved was to have some peace and quiet and some space and be away from the casserole ladies. That is the name everybody gives them. The widows who bring around casseroles to men who are suddenly single. But it appears, I didn't move far enough away."

"Sure!" said Katie jokingly.

"It's true. But Katie, all kidding aside, I kept meaning to tell you how much I loved and appreciated your art last night. It was so insightful, it took my breath away."

"Thank you Jack, I loved painting those. Let me paint one for you?"

"Wonderful. I would really like that." He smiled at her. "Would you like to go for a walk on the beach after breakfast?"

"Yes." She pointed out toward the sea. "Look at the beautiful sailboats. I love boats."

"One day we will have to go sailing."

After breakfast, they walked and talked for hours. As they headed back to the cottage, Jack saw two strangers in suits standing on top of a nearby hill. When he returned to the cabin, the phone rang, it was Danny.

"Hi Dad. I have been trying to reach you since yesterday. I was worried. Everything okay?"

"Everything is good Danny, very good."

Katie pointed to her watch indicating it was time for her to leave.

"Hold on Danny, I'll be right back." He kissed her saying, "I'll call you later, okay?"

"Perfect." She kissed him on the cheek and walked on clouds as she made her way to her car.

"Who was that?"

"Someone you don't know, Danny. A new friend I met. She is very nice, you would like her."

"Is that so? And here I was concerned you sounded so lonely the last time I talked to you. Strange world isn't it?"

"Yeah, talk to you later Danny, got lots of errands to run. Love you."

"Love you too, Pop."

Jack showered, dressed in his everyday khakis, donned a polo shirt and his trusty comfortable sneakers but he was still thinking of the night before with Katie. He was glad that she had come over and now that she was gone, he missed her. She had a great sense of humor and a special laugh.

Jack dialed his attorney, Henry Weismann, from the car as he stopped at a stoplight.

"Hank, talk to me, what did you find out about that eviction sticker on my door?"

"It looks like a mix up in the housing department but it has been hell to get them to rescind it. I am still working on the property tax auction but it does not look good. I have not been able to get anyone to budge at all. And our hearing has been moved up to this coming Friday."

"Oh great, just what I need. Keep working on it."

"Jack, don't worry about the eviction sign. I think I have that under control. The other problem will take some time."

Jack noticed while sitting at the stoplight, a rather large man get out of the car stopped next to him and walk toward him. The big man pulled back the windshield wiper with great force and shoved a yellow piece of paper underneath it. He stood glaring at Jack before walking away. It was one of the goons from the other night. He tried to get the license plate number but it was no use.

Jack turned the corner and got out of the car, with traffic whizzing by him, and pulled out the yellow sheet placed there by the mountain of a man. It was a page from the yellow pages, a list of local moving companies. It was a not so subtle hint for Jack. He was running out of time.

Chapter Twenty-Six

Katie called Jack an hour later. "Hi, I just called to say hello. I thought my art class was supposed to start today but it is for next week. I am glad I hired Jessie to help organize things for me."

"Does that mean you have the day free?"

"Yes, but I have a thousand things to attend to. Why, what did you have in mind?"

"Join me for a picnic lunch?"

"Well I don't know. I will have to think about it," she said, playing hard to get. "Okay you talked me into it."

He laughed. "I'll be by at eleven o'clock to pick you up. See ya."

Precisely at eleven, Jack was outside the gallery building and double parked the car on the side lot. Katie saw him from inside and rushed to greet him, kissing him as he held her in his arms.

"Where have you been all of my life," she exclaimed.

"Here," he said simply, "right here."

She jumped into the front seat. "I love picnics! Where are we going?"

"It's a surprise."

"That's even better—a picnic surprise."

They made their way east towards the ocean and then headed north towards the Boynton Beach inlet. The place was jammed with wall to wall beachgoers.

"Here? Not a lot of privacy," Katie said out loud, eyeing the multitude of people coming and going.

"I said it was a secret." Jack smiled at her. "You are not going find out that easy." He grabbed the picnic basket he prepared for their lunch as he took her hand and walked through the parking lot, past the beach goers, the restaurants, until they reached the edge of the marina. He stopped in the small wooden shack at the beginning of the pier before they made their way towards the waiting sailboats. Jack jumped into the beautiful J Boat docked at a nearby berth and stowed the picnic basket.

"Here let me help you aboard." He offered her his hand.

"What? Whose is this?"

"It belongs to a very close friend. I gave it to him a number of years ago with the understanding he will let me use it when the occasion arises. Hop aboard!"

She loved taking boat rides and loved watching sailboats but had only been on a beautiful boat like this once before. Jack untied the lines securing the boat to the pier and soon they were motoring their way out of the safety of the harbor and heading out to sea. Once beyond the confines of the harbor Jack released one of the sails and it gently began filling with air.

Katie was in love again. The sail began to pull them away from the shore further out to sea, heading south. The boat surged under Jack's firm hand as air rushed to push the billowing sails.

"Come here, take the wheel," Jack said.

"Me? Jack, I don't know anything about sailing."

"I'll be right here next to you but I want you to experience the feeling of sailing. It is unlike any other feeling I have ever felt."

She slid next to him, taking the oversized wheel in her hands. She could feel the energy and the power of the sail as the water splashed on the side of the boat, spraying the air. The water rushed below her with the sails begging for more, pushing harder and harder.

Jack proceeded to open all of the sails, then the big, beautiful main sail unfurled right before her eyes and the jib blustered out before them, announcing their approach to the world. This was heaven. The sleek racing J-boat leapt in the water when the wind filled the topsails the other sails joined in a dance with the wind. Jack was right, it was like no other feeling she had ever experienced.

She settled into her seat and began to feel the nuances of the boat, with slight shifts she could gain more speed, a shift to the right would slow them down. When the wind changed direction Jack hustled to the trim the sails to redirect them for maximum performance.

They continued to sail south and soon a small island appeared ahead of them as she reluctantly let Jack once again take control of the wheel.

"The island ahead is a small coastal island named Kikkoman after the old ancient mariner," Jack told her as he dropped anchor just off shore. They were on the windward side of the island, shielded from the rising gusts of winds and allowing them to drift at anchor. The huge white clouds began to paint the sky.

"How's this for a quiet picnic spot?"

"This is perfect. Just perfect. Everything is perfect!"

He opened the picnic basket and spread out a blanket on the cramped rear quarters of the boat with the wind gusting, cooling the afternoon to a perfect temperature. Jack had prepared a feast of tapas for them to enjoy and produced the obligatory bottle of champagne.

"Jack, tell me about the book you wrote. I feel like such a clod, I never asked anything about yourself yet you know all about me. Is it going to be published?"

Jack smiled. "Soon. It is about a portion of my life which I felt I just had to write about before I could move on. I needed closure. Have you ever had something in your life that you found you had to talk about in order to let it heal?"

"Yes, I did, my divorce. But instead of writing a book, I spent a fortune in therapy before I could honestly say I was not the problem. It was the jerk I was married to for all of those years who was the issue."

"Well this book was my therapy. Originally I wrote it without the intent to publish it. I wrote it for me. My writing has always been intensely private to me and to share it with anyone else was beyond anything I could imagine." Katie squirmed a little on the blanket, thinking of his private letters she read. *What would he say if he knew she'd read them?*

Jack continued, "But writing the book was very therapeutic. And since I did not plan on publishing it or anyone else even reading it I could be incredibly candid." He raised the bottle from the bait bucket he was using as his improvised bucket of ice. "More champagne?"

"Sure," she said, glad to be off the proverbial hook. Sooner or later she knew she would have to say something to him about the letters. They were too personal to dismiss. Maybe he did not understand what she was talking about when she asked him about the letters. But now it was the letters that brought them together- today was not the day.

"We may get some rain," Jack said, looking toward the Western sky as a seasoned sailor eyeing the massing clouds.

"How did your book come before a publisher's attention?"

"You see my son Danny is a literary agent and while trying to explain some things to him I became tongue tied and unable to express myself, so, instead I had him read the book. It said it all. He liked it and pestered me to edit it and shop it around for a publisher. The rest is history."

"You said your book is about a period of your life, do mind sharing what happened with me?"

Jack paused, looked down before looking into Katie's eyes saying, " It is still difficult for me to talk about but I guess with the book coming out everyone will know. A number of years ago I was a physician practicing with the organization called Doctors Worldwide International. Well, while I was with them I had something happen which changed my life forever. You see…"

The crack of thunder just behind them interrupted him and was followed by an onslaught of wind and sheets of rain, sweeping over the boat drenching them. "Get inside, quick," he told her. "I'll grab everything here."

"Boy that was sudden" Katie said as she rushed down the steps with Jack right behind her.

"Unfortunately, the rain knows no barriers. The island will block the wind but not the rain. It was raining harder now, buckets of rain crashed against them.

The door into the cabin was stuck. Jack pushed and pushed as the rain poured down on top of them soaking their clothes until it the door finally opened. They were both dripping wet from head to toe with rain forming small pools of water at their feet.

"Let me grab some towels," Jack said. "You're drenched. We need to get you out of those wet clothes."

"Best offer I've had all day," she said lifting off the soaked t-shirt. The growing pile of wet clothes lay at their feet as he Jack kissed her and pulled her close. They held each other while the storm outside raged on and on, rocking the boat while inside, safe and dry they found pleasure in the wonderful silence of the rain and the storm while they made love to the seductive sound of raindrops.

As the days passed they would spend many afternoons together, picnicking on the sleek sailboat, making love or walking on the beach or searching the small antique stores of Delray. And as long as they were together, that was all that mattered to them. They were becoming closer and closer.

Chapter Twenty-Seven

Jack went by his attorney's office and stopped by the bank. He heard the same story from each. "It is not right them taking ownership of your house but it will take a while to straighten out the mess."

"Can't we file suit to delay them taking it?" Jack asked his attorney.

"No, Palm Beach County legal system does not work that way. Your only hope is to have a sympathetic judge in your corner at your hearing. Then just hope for the best. It is in his hands."

They all had the same story. He needed a miracle.

Jack continued to debate with his publisher about the book signing tour. He was not crazy about traveling, not now. He really did not want to travel much since he had found a reason to stay in Delray, Katie. But he knew that sooner or later he would have to go on the road.

But I may not have a house to stay in anyway if he could not find a way to block the final auction. The situation was bad. He drove to his final desperate last hope, the County Assessor's Office.

The Assessor's Office was filled with people waiting in three different lines. Some had appointments but others did not. The line stretched around the office with children crying and running about, using the tax office as their playground. A middle aged husband and wife were standing behind him arguing about who had forgotten to pay the tax bill. "Damn," he yelled at her, "if you had done what you were supposed to do we wouldn't be in this mess."

"Well, big shot, if you had put some money in the bank account, the checks would not have bounced. Stop spending all of our money on booze and buying everyone drinks at Mickie's and we would have some of our money left over for bills."

"Our money? Listen to me girl, I work fifty hours of week down at the truckin' terminal and if—"

"Next!" shouted the clerk at the counter, over the din of waiting people, all talking at the same time.

"Name," he shouted, as Jack approached the counter.

"Petersen, John Petersen. I have an appointment to see Ms. Bertram. It is on an appeal."

"Time?"

"My appointment is for two-thirty."

"Wait here, and I will check with her," said the skinny blond haired clerk with a severe case of acne.

Jack watched him disappear behind the counter. He stood looking out over the mass of humanity assembled in the tax offices. The clucking din of ten different languages brought back to Jack what his father had always said, "Jack my son, this is America, the melting pot, the land of opportunity."

"Dr. Petersen, Dr. Petersen, right his way, please."

He saw the same lady he had seen before, Ms. Bernice Bertram, Head Assessor.

"Good morning, Dr. Petersen, so nice to see you again. I did some checking on your appeal and your are correct, the bank did forward the disbursement to the processing center. But for some reason the processing center failed to remit their payment to us in due course. They did, however, send it in yesterday."

"Well, that's great. Wow! So that should take of it the problem, right?"

"Well no, Dr. Petersen. The auction still stands until it can go through our appeal process and until that time, they can legally tear down your house and proceed with their construction. They do have to wait until after your final appearance before Judge Kirk. If you can convince him, you may have a chance, a slim chance but it is still a chance." Jack felt dejected, this is not what he wanted to hear.

"I'm sorry Dr. Petersen but as I told you before this land is yours but it will take some time for the County to go through its process to prove it. That is just our bureaucracy. You can't even file suit to delay it, I am afraid. I am so sorry. But I do thank you for coming in to visit the Country Assessor's Office. Have a good day." She shook his hand and closed up her desk, she was finished for the day at three o'clock.

He headed home and called Katie on the way. "Can you get away and join me for dinner?"

"Sure, I was hoping you would call. What time?"

"Say seven?"

"Sure sounds great. See you then."

He called for reservations at Testas' in Palm Beach and thought they would drive up the coast, a nice romantic ride with the ocean as their traveling companion.

His phone rang, it was Katie. "Hey Jack, Jessie came in early and I can be there sooner if you like. I can't wait to see you." She was excited about spending the evening with him again.

"Sure come on over. Let yourself in if I'm in the shower. See ya then."

Jack ran up the steps when he got home and threw off his clothes tossing them to the floor and jumped into the shower. He draped the towel around him as he shaved, humming an unlikely tune. He heard a knock at the front door and remembered he forgot to unlock it.

"I'll be right there, Katie." He clamored down the steps two at a time and as he flung the door open expecting to see Katie, he was greeted by his former neighbor, Ginny. His smile faded and was replaced by a sense of embarrassment.

"Well you look like you are ready for action, Jack. Good to see you too," she said with a grin.

Jack clutched his towel tighter. "I thought you were someone else."

Then he heard a car door slam, and a familiar voice holler, "Hey Jack, I'm here!" It was Katie.

Jack glowered at Ginny. "What are you doing here?"

"I came to pick up my casserole dish and see maybe if we could get together, you know and try to make a go of it but it appears that I am already too late. Damn, all the good men are taken." She kissed him on the cheek and said, "Goodbye Jack."

Katie walked up the steps behind them as he said, "Goodbye Ginny."

The two women passed on the steps exchanging only a glance and a hello.

"Who was that?" Katie held a bottle of champagne in her hand and a glower on her face.

"It's not what you think," Jack said, shifting uncomfortably on his feet. He knew how it looked.

"Yeah? *I leave and come back and find him in nothing but a towel wrapped around your waist with some buxom blonde woman leaving his house. How dumb does he think I am?*

"What am I supposed to think? You tell me?" *I thought we had something special, something magical. Now I am not so sure what the hell is going on.* She turned to walk away but Jack held her arm and turned her towards him.

"Katie please let me explain," Jack pleaded. "Please."

"I'm listening. This I gotta hear. Go on," she said, tears welling in her eyes at his betrayal.

"That was Ginny the lady that left the casserole on my front porch. We used to be neighbors where I lived before. She wanted more of a relationship that I was willing to give her. I heard a knock on the door and thought it was you. Katie, we have known each other only for a short time but I feel very close to you, closer than I felt to anyone in a very long time." Brushing away her tears he pleaded, "Katie, please don't leave. Please."

She was angry and confused. She wanted to be with him so much but she had been hurt many times before and the feelings of betrayal all came rushing back to her.

Before she could say anything else, he whispered from his heart, "Katie, trust me. I will never, ever lie to you. My wife and I had a saying if something was the god's honest truth, with no joking…, we would say Emmis. No lies, no deception. I am what I say I am and what you see here standing before you is the best I can offer." His sincerity was so soulful and truthful, she had to believe him.

She said one word, "Emmis?"

"Emmis. What do you say we stay in tonight, okay?" He kissed her and pulled her close

"Yeah. Let's just stay here."

Two sets of peering eyes eased closer to the window, watching, waiting.

• • • • •

The big dark sedan pulled over to the shoulder just past Jack's house, it was well after two a.m. One man opened the car door and walked silently around the rear of his house and could soon be seen running back to his car, before the tires peeled away, driving fast down A1A.

• • • • •

Jack and Katie lay in bed still in that relaxed after lovemaking aura, when Katie suddenly asked, "What time is it? Is it sunrise already? It looks so bright outside, look!"

He was slow to wake, then looked outside. "That is not the direction the sun comes up, that is the rear of the house. It looks like something is on fire! Quick, get dressed." Duke, now awake, barked at the commotion. "You're a big help now, boy." Jack jumped out of bed and yanked on a pair of pants. "Call the fire department, quick." He ran down the steps, grabbed the hose from the side of the house and was greeted by an inferno engulfing his car. The Mercedes was now a huge bonfire. The water he sprayed on the firestorm had little effect. Katie came up beside him holding his arm.

"Kate, get me the keys to your car. I'm going to move it in case mine explodes."

She ran back into the house and was back in seconds with the keys.

"Now, run to the beach, quick before it explodes."

The sound of sirens soon pierced the silence of the night air, with the flashing yellow, red and blue lights bouncing off the trees and automobiles as they passed by, lending an eerie glow to the whole scene. The car was soon a pile of charred, smoldering metal, dead in the driveway.

"What do you think happened?" Katie asked, standing beside him, as the last of the flames were extinguished and the fire trucks pulled away.

"I think I have a pretty good idea of what happened and who did it. Somebody wants my property pretty bad and they will stop at nothing to get it," Jack said, still looking at his burned out Mercedes. "They were trying to burn me out."

"Who wants your house? What's going on?"

"Some out of town developers are trying to steal my property in order to build their condo buildings and it appears that they will stop at nothing in order to do it."

"But why would they burn your Mercedes?"

"To send me a message, Katie, and that message is, move. Well, it's not going to work, I'm staying put."

• • • • •

In deserted downtown Delray behind the new gallery, the watcher was waiting. He had found a new place to secret himself where he could watch her and spy on her from the darkened cluster of Mangrove trees behind her new apartment.

He had been rebuffed in his opportunity to charm her at the grand opening but now she would have to listen to him. He finally gave up at three a.m., realizing that his beloved Katie was not coming home that night so he would be back tomorrow and soon she would beg him to get back together.

"It's always tomorrow with her. But I'll be back," he growled. He left his hiding place and went to his car, some five-hundred feet away. When he turned the ignition when he felt the cold steel of a pistol at the base of his neck. He was pulled from his thoughts of having his way with his Katie again.

"Richard Kosgrove?" the voice from the rear of the car demanded.

"Who are you? What do you want? Money? My wallet is in my back pocket. Take it and leave, please." he pleaded.

"I said…, are you Richard Kosgrove?" the irritated voice asked a second time from the rear.

"Yes… I am. Who… are you? What… do you want?" he asked the man in the rear of the car, the terror totally evident in his voice, his pants wet with fear.

"Shut up and drive."

Chapter Twenty-Eight

"The Senate Subcommittee on Coastal Affairs is adjourned for lunch and will resume its deliberations and hearings at two this afternoon. Adjourned." The gavel hit the small block of dark walnut sitting on the Chairman's desk and Senator Swartzkopf set aside the gavel and walked down the white marble hallway leading to his office.

"Senator, your twelve-thirty appointment is here," said longtime aide, Meg. "There are two really sinister looking men waiting for you in the anteroom, Senator. Mr. Victor Scarlari and a Mr. Igor Krushevnsky. Who are these guys, Senator?"

"Just some associates, Meg. You know we must have consideration for all of our constituents, now don't we?"

"Yes, I guess so, Senator. But these guys look creepy."

"Meg, give me a minute to get in my office and then show them in, okay?"

"Yes, Senator."

The senator hurried into his office and settled into the large leather chair behind his desk. He glanced over his desk to make sure no sensitive documents were visible and checked the newest addition to adorned his desk, a large glass ball, a commendation from the firefighters of New York. Everything was in order; he was ready.

"You may show the gentlemen in now, Meg," he said through his intercom.

The two big men followed behind her and sat down in the chairs in front of his desk. His aide discreetly exited, shutting the door as she exited.

"Senator, it is so good to see you again," said Krushevnsky setting a leather briefcase besides his desk. Abe eyed the case for just a brief moment, before returning his attention to the two men.

"You know I don't like meeting here, in my office," he told them in hushed tones.

"I know Senator, but so many other places have prying eyes and ears. Here we can have complete privacy."

"Did you bring the money?" he asked.

"Right here, Senator," said the big Russian, patting the briefcase.

"Well, I certainly don't mean to rush you but I do have a subcommittee to run today."

"Yes, Senator, we know and that is precisely why we are here today, to make sure you vote against any further restrictions being placed on coastal development." The Russian lifted the brown leather briefcase and placed it on the Senator's desk.

"And we are paying a lot of money for that privilege Senator," interjected the brash Scarlari. The Russian turned to him quickly and quieted the upstart with a frown before proceeding.

"Senator this is just our way of saying that we endorse your reelection and know that due to some restrictive campaign finance laws you cannot accept all of the donations you deserve. We would like to make this small donation from me and my associates both here and in New York."

"Well, if you think five-hundred grand is small potatoes, Igor, I would love to see what you consider big," chortled Scarlari. Once again the Russian's frown stilled the tongue of Scarlari.

"Open it," the Russian invited the senior Senator. "It's all there, just as you requested."

Abe stood and turned the briefcase on its side, popping the gold latches which cracked the descending silence on the room. He opened the brief case. Rows and stacks of cash, all bundled and bound together, looking so fresh, as if they'd just came from the Treasury. Abe let out a small gasp at the sight of all the money sitting before him.

"Thank you, gentlemen. This will go a long way towards my reelection campaign," he said, without taking his eyes off the contents of the briefcase.

"Well Senator, we know you are a busy man, so we will not take up any more of your valuable time. We have plane to catch for Miami." He extended his hand to the Senator, who shook it vigorously. When they were gone, Abe sat in his chair admiring the cash that lay before him. Looking at it he smiled and said, to the round glass orb, "Done?" Now he could attend to his friend Jack Petersen.

Chapter Twenty-Nine

The private jet set down smoothly and rolled unobserved to the executive jet terminal at Miami International Airport. The sleek gold and white corporate plane was greeted at the tarmac by two large sedans with darkened windows and waited patiently in the hot Florida afternoon sun for the arrival of its VIPs onboard.

Igor Krushevnsky and Victor Scarlari soon emerged from the sleek Whisperjet and were quickly whisked away to their downtown destination aboard the darkened limousines. They were here to finish the Dr. Petersen affair, as the big Russian termed it. It would all be over soon.

• • • • •

Jack Petersen sat on his porch alone luxuriating in the morning quiet; the only sounds the soft murmuring of the ocean. Katie left earlier to prepare for her class at her new art school. He smiled as he remembered her walking up the steps with the magnum of champagne and the look of fear from his new would be female suitor Ginny. He never saw her move so quickly in his life.

He drank another sip of coffee, picking up the local newspaper and reread the story about the smashing success of Katie's gallery. She had made the front page! She looked so good being interviewed by Sara Reinhardt.

Jack looked out upon the water, noticing the noisy seagulls bickering and massing overhead and saw an enormous school of leaping fish passing right before his beach house. The fish were being chased by a school of hunting grey reef sharks just off the shore who were truly enjoying a movable feast. He could not believe his eyes. He'd never seen anything like it! He set down his coffee mug on the newspaper and then ran inside to grab his camera so he could document this unbelievable sight.

He ran to the beach, following the spectacle, clicking his camera one frame after another. There were fish swimming and jumping everywhere, some were desperately trying to reach the safety of the beach to escape the jaws of the hungry sharks. The camera clicked rapid fire photos of the group moving down the beach as he moved in tandem with them. The seagulls circling overhead joining in a cacophony of voices, at their new found food fortune. Then just as quickly as the food feast started, it was over, the only evidence was the continuing feeding of the hungry seagull scavengers.

Jack trudged back towards the cottage on the cool sandy beach reviewing his photos on the camera. He stopped walking, remaining frozen in front of his cabin.

The answer to how to save his home from the court proceedings the next day was right before his eyes. He zeroed in using his telephoto lens on the scene before him, excited about his discovery. He snapped five photos of the intruders before they fled as he hurried inside the cabin, only to find it had been ransacked. All the furniture had been turned over, looking as if they were searching for something. Or that someone had a fight inside his beach cottage.

"What the…" Jack muttered, never finishing his sentence. A club raised high over behind him, struck the back of his head, turning out the lights to his consciousness and he crumbled to the floor.

Jack didn't know how long he laid there or what caused him to wake. He didn't know if it was the sound of the approaching police sirens or Duke's wet tongue, licking his face. Either way he awoke with the worst headache imaginable. When he finally did open his eyes he saw, lying in his line of sight across from him, a dead man with a frozen stare. Jack felt the cold steel of a large caliber pistol in his hand.

"Don't move, this is the police," came a voice from behind him. "Release your hand from the weapon real slow like and move away from it, now! Do not make any sudden movements."

Jack released the pistol from his grip and tried to stand. Someone grabbed his hand from behind and a knee wedged itself in the middle of his back. "Give me your other hand and don't try anything funny, do you hear me? Stand up. Hey Joe, look at the gash on the back of this guy's head. The other guy on the floor is dead but his one is going to need the paramedics. Call an ambulance."

It was only then Jack realized what was happening—he was being framed for the dead man's murder.

The young cop began with a familiar refrain, "You have the right to remain silent, If you give up these rights…"

Realizing that things may not be exactly what they appear, the police set Jack down on one of the overturned chairs. Jack saw the full face of the dead man lying in his living room, it was the man who had hugged Katie at her grand opening—her ex-husband, Richard.

"Who is this guy?" asked the young cop with a pad, jotting down information.

"His name was Richard, Richard Kosgrove," Jack replied solemnly. "He was married to the woman I've been seeing."

"Is that so?" asked the cop, eager for more information. "Did you have a fight with the guy before you murdered him?"

"No! I didn't murder him! I didn't murder anyone! I want to speak to my lawyer."

• • • • •

The news of Richard's death hit Katie hard, harder than she ever thought it would. They'd been married for over fifteen years and she still had some feelings for him and for their marriage. She remembered the good times they had together right after they were married. She remembered the trips they took to Europe and the places they visited. She would mourn his death but most of her love had been drained after she found out about all of his numerous affairs. Still, she was shocked by the news of his death.

When she heard that Jack was being questioned concerning the death she was totally bewildered especially when she learned the death occurred at his beach home right after she had left his bed.

Jess walked into her office and set down a coffee. Kate glanced up at her best friend. Her eyes burned and her throat constricted.

"Jessie, did you hear the news? Richard was killed last night."

"I just heard about it." Jess came around Katie's desk and hugged her. "My god he was just here, I can't believe it. I was not one of his biggest fans but this is shocking. I can't—"

"Excuse me, ma'am, I'm with the Sheriff's department."

Jess pulled away and Katie stared at the officer who'd just interrupted them.

"I would like to ask you some questions about the death of your ex-husband, Richard Kosgrove," said the young dark haired detective. They were so engrossed in their conversation they had not heard him come into the gallery. He appeared much too young to be a seasoned cop.

"Yes, officer? Please come in. What can I tell you?"

"Was there any animosity between your ex-husband and Dr. Petersen that you are aware of?"

"No, none," she told him. "Richard, my ex, had just returned to Florida a couple of days ago. I had not seen him in over a year, not since our divorce became final. He just showed up here for the new opening of my store."

"Do you know a Dr. John Petersen?"

"Yes, we have been seeing each other recently."

"Was he here at your grand opening ?"

"Yes he was."

'At the same time as your ex-husband?"

"Yes, but I don't think he even met him that night. Richard had a lot of enemies in New York because of the many questionable real-estate deals he was always doing."

Jack could not be responsible for Richard's death. That was just not like him at all. Jack was willing to step aside when he saw Richard at the Gallery that night. No, she knew he could not have been involved.

Katie looked out into the street and saw a couple riding bikes down Atlantic Avenue. When they'd first been married, she and Richard, enjoyed riding bikes on the beach, going out to dinner and spending time together.

"Excuse me…, ma'am?" The young police detective interjected.

"Yes? I'm sorry officer, just idle thoughts I'm afraid. Anything else?"

"Do you know of any reason why anyone would want to kill your ex-husband?"

"No officer, not really. I've been out of his life for the last year. Richard was involved in a lot of controversial real-estate deals, but I guess he was well liked by most people."

"Most?"

"Well he lived in the rough and tumble world of international real-estate and he may have made enemies at some point in his career. But I'm afraid you'll have to talk to his office in New York if you want more detailed answers."

"One last question ma'am, you spent the evening with Dr. Petersen? He was with you until what time? Was he with you the morning of the murder?"

"Yes, officer. We are romantically involved and we spent the whole night together until approximately seven the next morning when I left him at his house and came here."

"Thank you for your time ma'am. We may be back in touch if we have any further questions."

"I'll be right here, officer. I am not going anywhere and I'm happy to oblige and help out any way I can. Is Dr. Petersen in jail? Where can I visit him?"

"He is still being interrogated at central police booking ma'am and he is not allowed any visitors except for his legal counsel. I'm sorry."

When the officer left the gallery, the silence returned and for some reason the tears welled in her eyes over Richard's death. She wasn't married to him anymore but that was no reason someone had to murder him. She sobbed, pausing to look around the studio, before pulling herself together and making a decision. *Now I have to see how I can help Jack out of his mess.* She picked up the phone.

Chapter Thirty

Jack spent the whole day and most of the evening being questioned by detectives about his role in the murder. He was tired, he needed a shave, a shower and desperately wanted to change his clothes. But more importantly, he was stressing out about being confined in a cell, which was particularly noted by the jail keeper and reported to the higher ups. Jack's attorney was getting nowhere with his requests for bail. Jack did not want to be in a cell, he wanted out and he would do anything to get out.

The next morning an older detective, who Jack had first spoken with when he came into the precinct office, walked into the interrogation room and set a folder on the desk between them.

"How you holdin' up there, Doc?" he said with a small grin.

Jack merely looked at him, without saying a word. Time passed and he responded tiredly, "I would like to leave."

"Well Doc, you may get your wish." The old detective opened the folder and looked up at Jack before beginning, "I have the results of all of the interviews we have conducted and the results of the crime lab or as they say on television, CSI. By the way, CSI does not solve crimes, they merely gather forensic information and turn it over to us detectives to investigate. Television, ugh! Those shows make my job so much tougher. Nowadays everyone thinks they are an expert."

Jack lifted his head and interrupted the detective to ask, "You said something about me being able to leave here, officer?"

"Oh yes, sorry. I do ramble on at times. We talked to someone who can collaborate your whereabouts at the time of the murder. The autopsy shows that someone went to great lengths to try to frame you for this murder. They injected Mr. Kosgrove with a sedative with a plan to shoot him and leave him in your house, with you holding the gun. What they did not know is, that Mr. Kosgrove had an extreme allergic reaction to this particular strong sedative and died soon after it was administered. His cause of death was from the sedative not from the gunshot and the coroner pinpointed his death at a time when Ms. Kosgrove was with you as your alibi." He paused to let it all sink in for Jack's benefit.

"You see Doc, rigor mortis had already started to set in when they shot him in your cabin and tried to frame it on you—he was already dead." The big cop stopped, obviously enthralled by his own voice.

"We thought initially maybe you and his ex-wife were in on it, you being a doctor capable of obtaining and administering a sedative. Then we heard from the Feds that they had some people of interest under surveillance and linked them to the murder. I can't go into anymore details but suffice it to say they cleared you of any wrong doing. So Doc, all charges have been dropped and you are free to go."

Jack shook his hand and was out the door after he stopped to sign the mountains of paperwork required for his release. He had a court hearing to get to and he didn't pick up his new car yet. He needed to get his camera and do it all quick, he knew he did not have a lot of time. When he stepped outside into the Florida sunshine, his spirits lifted. Katie stood there waiting for him.

"I am so sorry about Richard," he said holding her close, stroking her hair. "But I had nothing to do with his murder, Kate."

"I know, Jack. It hit me harder than I thought it would. For so many years he was a big part of my life and now he's dead. And I don't know why."

"I think I am beginning to understand why all of this is happening, Come on I'll tell you in the car. I need to get home first and then get to a court hearing as soon as possible. I need your help."

"Let's go," she said, rushing towards her car.

Jack laid it all out for her, the lost property tax payment, the auction of the house, the last court hearing, the late night ride with the big goons, the car fire and now, Richard's death. He told her how he thought they were all related.

When he got home he grabbed his camera, ran up the steps, showered, shaved and within fifteen minutes was ready to go. He had a crucial court hearing to attend.

Chapter Thirty-One

The courtroom was packed as Jack and Katie found a seat towards the rear. He scoured the room for his opponents until he saw them, sitting near the front beside the same skinny little man, with glasses. He must be the attorney for all of them, thought Jack.

Scarlari and Krushevnsky conferred together in a tight huddle, gesticulating with their hands as the bailiff walked to the center of the hearing room and addressed the courtroom. "All rise for the Honorable Judge Howard T. Kirk, presiding. The court will now come to order." *It was the same judge*, thought Jack.

Six cases were heard before Jack's name was called. The skinny little lawyer with the bowtie had joined the podium in four of the six cases. They were all found in favor of Scarlari, just as before. Jack was beginning to doubt whether his new strategy was going to work, but it was all he had in an effort to save his cottage.

"Mr. John A. Petersen, please step forward," said the large bailiff.

Jack walked past Scarlari and Krushevnsky and saw their sly grins, waiting for the inevitable. They were going to get what they wanted, one way or another and they wanted Jack's house.

"Dr. Petersen, here is the revised document that has been duly filed with the court correcting the legal name so it is now properly listed in our files. Please review this document and ensure this is now the proper spelling of your legal name, Dr. Petersen," said the smug judge.

"Yes, Your Honor, it is."

"Well if you have nothing more to add to this proceeding I will now make my ruling."

"I do, Your Honor."

"What? What do you mean?" asked the surprised and slightly irritated judge.

"I have something more I would like this court to take into consideration, Your Honor."

"Proceed, Dr. Petersen," said the now fuming Judge glancing at his watch. *I will never make my tee time now.*

"Your Honor, this property was originally found to be unbuildable and deemed a natural habitat for the endangered species of the South Florida Burrowing Owl."

The small, squeaky attorney quickly interjected, "Yes, that is true, Your Honor, but those owls have not been seen at that location in over two years. The temporary restraining order on building on that property was then voided at my client's request and signed by you, Your Honor."

"Yes, I understand a number of poisoned dead owls mysteriously appeared on the beaches a number of years ago," Jack said, facing the lawyer. "No one knows who poisoned them."

The judge cleared his throat and blurted out, "I recall the request and Dr. Petersen unless those owls have returned from the dead, I am afraid you are out of luck," said the red faced judge, eager to get on with the proceedings.

Jack opened the manila folder he had been carrying and gave it to the Bailiff who handed it to the judge. "Your Honor, I have not seen any of that evidence Mr. Petersen is providing to the court. May I please see that, Your Honor?"

"In due time Mr. Hatcher, in due time," the judge said and after examining it, he returned it to the Bailiff to give to the attorney.

"Your Honor, that is a picture taken on my front porch this morning of two nesting Burrow Owls, both alive and well. I had suspicions that someone or something was watching me the last couple of weeks but it was not until today that I was able to photograph them."

"Your Honor," protested Hatcher, "those photographs could have been taken years ago."

"Your Honor," Jack interjected, "if you will notice the front page photo is of a Ms. Katherine Kosgrove and a story detailing the opening of her new art gallery in downtown Delray Beach these past weeks. Ms. Kosgrove is here with me today to verify that information, should you so desire."

"That will not be necessary, Dr. Petersen. I have heard enough evidence in this case. I find that this property is to be returned permanently to the category of restrictive habitat and therefore unbuildable from this day forward. Case dismissed."

"But your honor, we have a bill of sale signed by Dr. Petersen agreeing to sell the property to us."

The judge peered over his bifocals and glared at the man challenging him, "I said this case is dismissed."

Katie hugged Jack, kissed him and said, "My hero. You should have been a lawyer."

They walked arm and arm from the hearing room, only to be stopped by the same big goons who had kidnapped Jack earlier.

"Not so fast Petersen," said Ivan, the biggest one. "Mr. Scarlari is going to want to talk with you, I am sure." He kept his hand in his suit pocket but the message was clear: *I have a gun, move and I will shoot you dead.*

Scarlari and Krushevnsky walked from the room behind them, their faces told the whole story, millions of dollars lost. They would have to tell their investors that their money and all of their profit was gone, all four-hundred million dollars worth. The IREC was not filled with forgiving people, especially when it came to large sums of money like this. All because of Jack Petersen and his burrowing owls.

"Dr. Petersen, we underestimated you. I would like you to join me for a short ride, both of you," he said, nodding to Katie. "Kiss her goodbye now, because you won't have lips left when I finish skinning you, my friend."

Knowing they were going to die, Jack looked at the thug and then at Katie. Pulling her close, he kissed her a kiss to last a lifetime. "I love you," he whispered in her ear.

"I love you too, Jack."

"All right, let's go you two love birds," said the big Russian, and Jack felt something hard pushing into his back, moving him along.

Suddenly, the corridor was flooded with men in dark suits, all with their guns drawn, pointed at the big Russian and his thugs.

"This is the FBI, hands in the air where we can see them, now!"

Their hands raised in compliance, bewildered at the surprise appearance of government officials. It was going to cost more money for bribes, just like in Russia, thought Krushevnsky.

"Now everyone on the floor, spread 'em and don't move."

They dropped to the cold white marble floor, bewildered as to what was happening to them.

"Are you okay," asked a curly red-haired FBI agent, his badge dangling from around his neck.

"Yes and you got here in the nick of time. Thank you," replied a grateful Jack.

The agent grabbed Scarlari and Krushevnsky and pulled them to their feet.

"I demand to know what is going on here. I pay my taxes and I am a law abiding citizen," said the big Russian.

"You have nothing on me," said Scarlari. "I demand to see my attorney."

"Yes, sir you will have plenty of time for that."

"What am I being charged with?" asked the big Russian.

"You are being charged with multiple counts of bribing a public official. We have on tape you and your associate here attempting to bribe Senator Abraham Swartzkopf. You will be charged with extortion, fraud, and failure to register as a foreign agent." The FBI agent was very thorough.

"You see the Senator and your administrative assistant, Meloris Katchkov, who is now under our protective custody, have been working with us for months to collect data on your criminal enterprise. We have a very nice video of you and Mr. Scarlari handing a bribe over to the Senator in his office."

"You got nothing on me," spewed Scarlari.

"We are adding one count of murder to your charges, Mr. Scarlari. We have you on film kidnapping a Mr. Richard Kosgrove."

Katie bristled when she heard who murdered Richard.

"You were the last person to see him alive and we have some wonderful DNA samples from the body which we have already matched to you. Mirandize them and take 'em away." The agent turned to his men, motioning them to whisk them away.

"We had to wait until we could get them both together," said the agent, "so the other one would not take flight and run. Sorry we could not do it sooner. We may need you testify about the property hearings but probably not for months. Have a good day now folks."

Katie and Jack watched him walk away, and her hand slowly reached for his, their fingers intertwined together. "Let's go. I want to hear the ocean at your place," she said kissing him.

"Yes, that sounds like a good idea." He pulled her close and kissed her again.

Chapter Thirty-Two

"Good morning, sleepy head," Kate whispered as she rolled over, placing her hand on Jack's chest. Katie loved to twirl the small wisps of hair on his upper body, spinning them into tight little circles before moving higher to stroke his ear. She prized touching him at this time in the morning. Laying there in his arms was her favorite time of the day.

Jack still looked asleep but grunted an acknowledgement. Weeks had gone by since the excitement at the courthouse and they'd grown closer together.

"Morning," he breathed, while she snuggled closer to him. She luxuriated in the masculine scent of his lightly fragranced musk aftershave—the scent of a man, her man. Their morning movement attracted the attention of their ever present companion, Duke. He waddled from his blanket in the corner of the room over to her bed, his tongue dripping with long gooey saliva and then strategically placing his head on top of the mattress. Eyeball to eyeball. Looking at her. He wanted to go outside.

Felix purred, still asleep in his usual spot underneath the bed. He was never far from them but liked to sleep in late, curled up until he heard Katie get up for breakfast. Food.

They had been up late the night before to attend an art exhibit, then went dancing and drove up the coast in Jack's new convertible sports car. Afterwards he decided to spend the night together at her place. She loved to dance with him, his leads of where he wanted to take her on the dance floor were so firm, as to leave little doubt where she was supposed to step next. She was sure she could talk him into going dancing again tonight. He issued a soft groan and went back to sleep.

"I am going to take Duke for his constitutional," she said, kissing his forehead and letting him sleep a while longer. "I'll be back soon."

He grunted in response, as she got up, dressed and grabbed her leash and doggie bag.

"Come on, Duke, let's go." She only had to ask him once and he was at the door waiting for her while she put on her cap.

The streets of Delray were just starting to wake. The trash trucks were busy picking up the piles of rubbish while the delivery trucks to the restaurants were already fast unloading their goods. Delray was waking up and coming alive! She walked to the park and waited while Duke inspected five different trees before picking a suitable location to mark his presence.

The traffic moved briskly along Atlantic Avenue. Retailers hosed down the sidewalks, preparing for another busy day of business.

Soon it was time to head back to her apartment. "Come on, Duke. You all done?" He tilted his head to the side in a curious fashion as if he did not understand the question. "I'll take that as a yes," she said, shivering from the cool front bringing the approaching rains. She glanced at the darkening skies overhead, it was going to storm again something fierce.

She ran up the steps to her apartment with the strong scent of Jack's Moroccan coffee filling the air, coupled with the drifting smell of bacon and eggs tickling her nose. Her stomach growled, she was hungry.

"We're back," she said, depositing her plastic bag into the trash container. She kissed Jack on the neck and patted his behind as she walked by. He was wearing his old Duke University t-shirt, stretched tight, hugging the muscles across his chest. She loved him in that t-shirt and he knew it.

"Morning," he said, while handing her a mug of freshly brewed coffee. She jumped up on the stool by the counter, watching him fry up the eggs with tarragon and Worcestershire sauce. She loved watching him, especially when he was cooking. For some reason food always seemed to taste better when it was cooked by someone else. And besides, Jack was a great cook.

"You all done your duty?" he asked Duke standing by his side. Duke barked, thinking he was being asked to go outside again. "No we are going to eat first, okay boy?"

"I'll set the table," said Katie, humming a tune. She grabbed the plates, silverware and napkins and set them on the table.

"Raytown is really coming alive at this time of day," she said with a cheery grin, while she carefully rolled the napkins around the knife and forks. She stopped when she heard a strange silence behind her.

She turned around and Jack was standing there, looking at her a frown on his face, his spatula raised in the air, motionless.

"What did you say?" he asked.

Katie paused, thinking for a minute, slightly alarmed. "I said, I'll set the table."

"No, after that what did you say?"

"Let me think. Oh, I said Raytown is really coming alive at this time of the day," and she turned, continuing her work in setting the table, humming the same tune she always hummed.

He walked behind her, clutching at her wrist, turning her to face him. "You said Raytown. Raytown? Where did you ever hear that? And that tune you keep humming? That tune is MacArthur Park. That was my wife's favorite song and she is the only person who ever referred to Delray as Raytown, until you did just now. Why is that so?"

The suddenness of his questions threw her off guard and the tone of his voice alarmed her. Katie was scared. Had she betrayed her closely guarded secret? She should have told him long ago about the letters. But now, like an approaching thunderstorm, her secret was coming out. Her world was about to come tumbling down around her.

A light went on in his eyes. "You read my letters, didn't you? You read the letters I wrote to Laura," he shouted, almost choking on the painful words. "Danny thought she saved them somewhere. You read them didn't you? All of the references to places I wrote about and things we did… you seemed to know. No wonder you knew so much about me, you read my letters. They were private. I thought it was strange at first and then I did not want to think about it. I pushed it out of my mind. You could only know these things as a result of reading my letters."

"Yes. Yes I did," she sputtered defenselessly, dropping her head in shame willing to accept whatever he had to say to chastise her. But it was finally out in the open… she was relieved of the burden at last.

The shock and disbelief registered on his face. She scrambled, not knowing what to say or how to save it. She was terrified, she knew where this was headed.

"You never said anything about finding any of my letters. Katie, I trusted you," he said in a tone of resignation.

"Jack, I was going to tell you, I tried to tell you at dinner that first night… but I never found the right time and then we became so close I didn't want to lose you." Tears began to fall down her cheek. "You thought I was talking about the money but I wanted to tell you about a finding the letters but you didn't want to talk about it. Jack, please, please listen to me. Let me explain." She looked up at him, but he averted her gaze, his eyes filled with pain and betrayal. He was done with her. That look pierced her soul. *Oh god, what have I done!*

"How could you?" he whispered. "How could you read something so personal, so private? Those letters were not meant for you," his voice quivered. His eyes and face contorted in pain, the realization of it all sinking into his psyche.

"Jack I found them in the books I bought from you in the flea market when we first met. I was going to return them to you, but..."

Jack wasn't listening. He grabbed his car keys, slapped his thigh to signal to Duke it was time to go. Duke was up in a flash but paused before following, looking at her, not sure if she was coming with them and whether he should stay or leave. Finally he turned and ran after his master. Jack was out the door and out of her life.

Katie was now all alone. Her home and her heart never felt so empty. It was so quiet, no laughter, no love, nothing but her empty soul. She wished now she'd burned the damn letters!

"No," she said out loud. "No, it can't be. I can't lose him. Not after all of this. He is part of me now." She ran down the steps, out into the street, running to the parking lot, only to find it empty. He was gone. The sharp pain of separation began to torment her already. She turned to go back inside, and she cried.

Chapter Thirty-Three

Kate called Jack as soon as she got back inside, but there was no answer on either his cell or his home phone, only his voicemail. She needed to talk to someone… she called Jessie.

"Give him some space for a couple of days, he'll be back," Jessie consoled her while they were having coffee later that morning.

"Jess, I'm afraid I really screwed it up this time. Those damn letters, I wish I'd never found them!"

"It will be okay, he really cares for you. Just give him a couple of days to sort it out and then go over to see him. It was just a shock to his system that's all. You guys can work this out, I'm sure of it."

Kate sighed, suddenly so unsure of herself. Jack's anger was so intense. She'd betrayed him. Was it something he could ever get past?

"I don't know… He was pretty angry. I betrayed him. I didn't mean to, honest. I feel so terrible inside."

"And that is exactly what you will tell him when you see him Katie, those exact words. Tell him you feel terrible and tell him you're sorry. Guys are just like us in that way, they like to hear the words. Just tell him you're sorry."

"I told him that already. I have to do something more, something to show that I never meant to hurt him."

"Katie, why didn't you just give him the letters before all of this happened? Or destroy the damn things so they would never come between the two of you? You know, clear the decks before it got to this."

"They were so much a part of him, of how we became close, I did not have the heart to destroy them and I was afraid if I gave them to him he would be so angry he would walk out on me."

"You mean like he just did? Katie go see him, tell him the truth, be honest with him. Trust me kiddo it is really the best thing to do."

Kate nodded. "Okay, maybe you're right. I will wait a couple of days and let him calm down and then go over to his place and talk to him."

"That's the ticket. Now just imagine the great makeup sex you are going to have when you tell him."

"Jess, you are incorrigible."

Her friend laughed. "I know."

The next couple of days around the studio and gallery were pure torture for Katie. She was just going through the motions of living a life. Saturday she woke bright and early and had her morning jog.

She showered, dressed in a low cut peasant blouse, her tight form fitting jeans, then got in her car. As she drove towards Jack's house, seeing the familiar landmarks along the way served to heighten the anticipation she was feeling. The thought of seeing him was exciting.

Over and over again in her head she thought about what she was going to say to him. The hell with it, she was just going to say how sorry she was and throw herself on his mercy. That should work, she hoped. The letters were tied in a neat bundle beside her on the seat of the car. It was well past the time to return them. *She would say how sorry she was and that she never meant to hurt him and they would make up. Then… yes, it would be great sex.*

Katie took a deep breath as she parked her car in his driveway. Peering through the garage windows she could see his car and began to shiver in anticipation. *Don't turn back now!* She made her way to the front door. Oddly, the porch chairs where they would sit in the morning and watch the sun come up were no longer there.

She took another deep breath and knocked on the door. The house remained silent, no noise came from the door latch being opened, no sound of Duke announcing the knock at the door. She knocked again. The only noise she heard was the sound of the ocean waves behind her, and the seagulls looking for their morning meal. There was no answer at the door.

The window curtains were slightly parted on the front porch and she glanced inside. All of the furniture was covered in large white sheets, looking something like a ghost town. The sight of it struck fear in her heart. In desperation she dialed his home number. There was no ring inside. A voice came on announcing it had been disconnected. She dialed his cell and received the same message. Her stomach dropped. He was gone. It was then she noticed the red and white *For Sale* sign posted on the front porch. He was truly gone. "Those damn letters," she said out loud and began to cry.

The next two months Katie lived and walked through life like a zombie, half dead and half alive. Jessie tried to help her out of it but it was of no use. Even her wonderful paintings had taken on a surreal dark foreshadowing. Jessie was concerned for her best friend.

"He will be back," Jessie said. "His car is still here, remember? He can't just leave it here. He has to come back for it. And he will be back for you too."

"But his house is up for sale. I have pushed him away. He'll never come back."

Katie drove by his house once a week or every ten days when she just happened to be in the neighborhood to check if his car was still there. That was her security blanket, the knowledge that as long as his car was there, he would return. He just needed time she told herself.

At night, after the gallery closed, she would read. She had finished reading all of her books stacked on the floor which constituted her must read pile. She had reread the poetry books of Allison White three times. She loved the intricacies of her writing and the passion in her elegant prose.

One evening, Felix squatted down on her pile of letters on her desk. She jumped to her feet, grabbing the letters from beneath him. The ribbon holding the letters together fell off and the letters tumbled to the ground. She picked them up one by one, slowly reliving the memories she had of each one. There were still some letters she had not read. They seemed to mock her now but she sought refuge in the words, anything to be near him, to hold him in her arms again. She knew she should not read them but could not help herself. She settled onto the sofa.

March, 2009

My Dearest Darling,

You always wanted to go to Greece and see the Parthenon, the Acropolis, the other Greek ruins and the Greek islands. Remember after we toured the area we snuck away from our group and went down the tiny little back alley ways in the Plaka section of Athens.

We found a quaint little Greek restaurant with nothing but locals and the menu was all in Greek. Remember they invited us into the kitchen and we pointed at all of the dishes we wanted while they were still cooking in a huge pots on the stove? I can remember the next day, a shop with a turning spit of roasted lamb at the little market on the corner. The *Souvlaki* there was the best in the world as he would carve it off a slice at a time. The food was so delicious. Do you remember?

The dancing that night was delightful to watch and they urged us on to learn their Greek dance. We danced on the tables until dawn. The wonderfully harsh taste of Retsina still returns to my mouth to this day, to remind me of how we danced the night away. The combination of the fantastic food, the music, the ouzo and the bouzouki was wondrous. Remember?

What was your favorite place? Remember Syros? Ah yes, Syros! Remember we... Sorry, I must go. Love you always.

Forever,

Jack

Katie felt like she was there with him in Greece. Looking out over the green blue waters of the Aegean Sea. She could smell of the sting of the salt air, she could see the old fishermen, feel sorry for the widows all dressed in black and the old men in the tavernas tossing their multi-colored worry beads, back and forth between their fingers. Yes, she felt she was there in Greece.

She picked up the next letter and began to read.

April, 2009

My Dearest Darling,

I heard a laugh the other day, then a shout, they were all speaking Greek. I don't know who it was, maybe one of the guards, but it brought back such memories of the times when we went to Greece. Remember my love?

Remember our trip to Syros my love? It took us many years to return to Greece and we decided to visit a new island but we finally did it for our anniversary.

Do you recall, the ferry we took from Piraeus and sailed the crisp blue Aegean Sea in search of our siren song, the small Greek island of Syros? We had always seen pictures of the beautiful island and you would always say that one day you wanted to go there. I had always promised to take you, to see its white washed buildings, the *omnipresent blue doors, the windmills on the top of the hills and the wild flowering Bougainvillea everywhere. Finally we made it.*

We fell asleep on the ferry only to be awakened hours later, by a blast of the ship's horn. We looked through the porthole in our cabin and saw the island swiftly retreating behind us, with its windmills on top of the hills.

Rushing to leave we jumped to the safety of the old wooden pier, laughing as we waved goodbye to the ship pulling away. Together we walked down the long pier and made our way into town only to find that the only hotel on the island had burned to the ground.

We had to board in the local convent, in separate single beds and in separate rooms. I so wanted to hold you that evening, to comfort you through your loss but I was denied. Until I saw you creep into my room. I held you close, closer than ever before. I wanted to hold you, to take your pain away but that we both now know pain only eases with time.

The three reflective days we spent on that tiny little island, waiting for the ferry to return were exactly what we needed. Time alone to grieve. The people there must have known of our loss and gave us our privacy as we grieved together. I will always remember those days for those days there were a salve to the soul.

It was so glorious and to see your occasional laugh again, it lifted my soul to its greatest heights. Your mother will always be missed, she was such a cherished friend to both of us. Our lives honor her memory.

My heart aches for you now my love, as I wish I could see your face, touch your skin and hear your laugh. Remember, always remember, my love.

I must go.

Forever,

Jack

Guards? What guards? What was Jack talking about? Who were the guards? What were they guarding? Were they guarding him? Now she was concerned. Had Jack been in prison? What crime did he commit? They put murderers in prison but she knew Jack could not be a murderer.

She called Jessie on her cell phone.

"Slow down. You don't know what it is or where he was, all you know is was Jack. You know Jack. Trust him. Hey remember, didn't you tell me Jack went into prisons with his medical group to give prisoners their medical care? That has to be it! Yeah, that has to be the guards he was talking about. Did you read the last letter? Maybe it will give you more information."

"There is a two month gap after this letter. I don't know if he did not write one or if it got lost but it was not in the ones I have here with me. But Jess I am afraid to read it now. After reading the last one about the guards, I don't know what to think."

"Kate, read the letter. You have come this far. Read it. Then call me, all right?"

"Okay, bye."

She placed the letter on her lap and began to read.

June, 2009

My Dearest Darling,

I miss you. I understand now the true meaning of the word yearn. My heart has ached for you as it has at no other time before. My hands and mind and all of my senses reach for you, reach for you to be there. I look to see you, touch you, and feel you but only with my mind. It is a feeling like no other. I yearn for you, I ache for you, I hunger and thirst for you with every molecule of my being. I can manage no other time. It is only with my memories that I will be able to quench my thirst for you. Dante's inferno is a mere candle to my flame, my desire for you. If only just to see you. I can wait no longer or else I surely shall die. I can no longer endure this pain, this hell. Remember my love, I am always here, always here for you.

My dearest, I never tire of saying those words, my dearest, I love touching you and holding you. I have touched this letter, held this letter close, closer than anything before and now you touch this same letter. Feel the love and desire. I am at my end, until next month, hold on my love, hold on. I miss you and love you more than words could ever say. I shall see you soon, my love. I can hardly wait. Remember me and always remember my love.

Forever,

Jack

This letter was different than the others from him that she had read. This letter was more urgent and heart wrenching. She wished she could have spoken to Jack to talk to him about the letters and the motivation behind them. She placed the letter with the others and again tied the ribbon around them. She missed Jack but she had come to the realization that she may never see him again. That thought was an arrow through her heart, a pain that only time would heal. She did not want it to heal, she wanted Jack. She welcomed the pain, it was the only thing which made her feel alive.

She thought of the last letter she'd read, untied the pile and pulled it out again to reread. The letter spoke of yearning, how he yearned for his wife, how he had missed her so much it struck a familiar bell and tone. She got up and pulled out her dogged ear copy of the last Allison White poetry book she had bought at the bookstore. She looked at the title, *Yearning and Remembrances* by Allison White. She flipped through the book, searching, desperately searching for a poem she had read. Then she found it, *Yearnings* and began to read again, with a new insight.

Yearning
My soul doest speak to chart thy journey for evermore
Oh how my troubled heart weeps, yearns and now aches for thee-
thy mysterys well so deep - thy soul begs me, come hither my love, come to me,
Quench my heart's desire - feel thy love, my love afire,
More depth unto my heart- chart thy journey for thust to meet -
What keepst my eyes to peace- oh my soul dost forever weep
I yearn for thee evermore, sweet light of yonder lore
The fire lights passion in my soul -
Forever lost without your light, forever cold but now so bold
I fear not the journey into the night
Even though you burn into mine own sight,
My love for thee whilst ever yearn
My soul should wander the darkest days, waiting, oh waiting for thy return…

It was almost as if the writer was responding to Jack's letters. This is crazy, Kate thought. Get a grip girl. You are going off the deep end.

She slowly opened the book to the dedication page, something she almost never got in the habit of reading.

This book is dedicated to my best friend, my lover,
my confidant, my lightening rod, my soul mate,
and if I search the globe forever but shall never find another like you,
you, my loving husband, Jack.
Totus Tuus
Allison

Katie remembered from her high school Latin the words *Totus Tuus* translated to *totally yours*. The author, Allison White was Jack's "Dearest Darling." His Laura was Allison White!

Now she was even more confused than ever. What had happened that these two could not be together? They were obviously so deeply in love. She took both the book of poetry and the letters and held them close falling asleep on her sofa. She should have never deprived Jack of his letters, his private thoughts to his wife, she thought as she drifted off to a troubled sleep. Now she understood.

Chapter Thirty-Four

Katie threw herself into her painting with a mad frenzy, the frenzy of a woman possessed. One Saturday, when she finished a painting in her studio, she called to ask Jess, "What do you think?"

"Well," responded Jessie, "it does show a different side of you, that's for sure."

"No, tell me what you really think of it. You are my best friend. Its crap isn't it?" she asked, taking a painters knife to the still wet canvas, slashing it to shreds. "Enough! Time for me to get back to painting things that I love. Time for me to get on with my life."

"That's my girl," responded Jessie. "Tell you what, I have a run to the bank to make a deposit, why don't you take a break and meet me for lunch at Maria's on Atlantic. I'll even let you buy. Just like old times."

"Okay," said Katie with a grin. "You got a deal."

She cleaned up the paint and decided to drive the ten blocks for lunch, and since she had the time, she'd drive by Jack's place. She drove the familiar route to his beach house and parked the car on the gravel driveway. The owls fluttered away in angst as she walked up to look inside the garage. Her heart sank. Jack's car was gone! It was no longer in the garage. And the *For Sale* sign was down. He was now truly gone.

Katie was devastated as she drove back into downtown Delray to meet Jessie. She knew it was going to come to this sooner or later, but she'd had hope. Now she faced the realization that Jack was gone, out of her life and the thought terrified her.

At night the local Maria's was a sports bar with the TVs carrying baseball, football, soccer, NASCAR and the like. During the day it did a thriving lunch business in pizzas, subs and wraps to the Delray business and tourist community. It was always a favorite with the locals and always busy.

Katie grabbed a table near the front of the store and kept an eye out for Jessie. She was still reeling from the knowledge that Jack's car was gone. She had to accept it. She ordered an ice tea from the young waitress handling her table.

The place was filling up fast while the young manager used the remote to change the channels on the TV nearest to Kate. The young fans began to chant, "Marlins, Marlins, Marlins!"

She could hear in her subconscious the verbal clips as he flipped through the channels, searching for the Marlins baseball channel.

The background noise ran in her mind as she heard him change the channels. "We are going to have another gorgeous day today in South Florida, sunny… The news from Washington- the Congress is still reeling from the influence peddling scandal… We will be joined today by Dr. John Petersen, author of the new book, *Captured*, right after this break… The Marlins take on the Yankees today in a game that you don't want to miss coming up right after this break…"

"Stop," she said almost screaming, to the young manager. "Go back to that last channel, please." He looked at her in startled amazement, while it took a second to register her request.

"Please," she repeated desperately. "Go back to that last channel, please."

His young nimble fingers retraced the channel selector back. "He will be joining us later in the show today to talk about his time spent…" They flashed a picture of Jack on the screen.

"Hey lady, we came here to watch the Marlins baseball game," said a guy with long hair and multiple tattoos seated with a group of nearby baseball fans.

"It's almost time for the first pitch," said the big one stuffed into a too small Marlins jersey.

Kate threw some money down on the table just as her tea arrived. "Keep it," she hollered, rushing out the door.

Katie drove home and turned on the TV, just in time to see Jack walk onto the stage to greet Matt Mohr and Susan Guilford, the hosts of *Good Day America*. He looked good, Katie thought, a little thinner but just as she remembered him. She missed him, she thought as he took his seat.

"We have as our guest today, the bestselling author, Dr. John Petersen. Welcome Dr. Petersen."

"Thank you, Matt and Susan, I am truly overwhelmed to be here with you and your nationwide audience."

"Dr. Petersen is the author of the recently released book *Captured* which is climbing the *Times* bestseller list. The book details his nearly three years spent in captivity at the hands of the Iranians. But I understand there is a lot more to the story than what a reader will see in these pages."

"Yes, there is Matt."

"But first tell me about the book and how it all happened."

"I was working as a surgeon in a group practice with an organization called Doctors International Worldwide, or DIW as everybody calls it. I was getting ready to retire early to care for my wife but I was also a military reservist."

"Your wife was ill, Dr. Petersen?" asked Susan.

"Yes, my wife had been diagnosed with Early Onset Alzheimer's at the age of forty-eight. I asked for a hardship release from the Marines but there was such a shortage of skilled physicians with my background that my request was denied."

He stopped for a moment to collect himself. "I was only supposed to be gone three weeks and since she had just been diagnosed I thought I would go and get it over with—come back quickly to spend all of my time with my wife. My wife and I were very close. As a matter of fact she worked as a nurse and many times she would accompany us on our DIW missions.

"On my three week reserve duty I was assigned to a Surgical Trauma Group heading to the Northern Iraq and the chopper hit some turbulence, which knocked out our guidance and navigation systems. We crash landed and I was the only survivor, the rest of the crew died in the crash. I was found later the next day by an Iranian military patrol. It seems our chopper had strayed across the Iranian border and they took me prisoner."

Katie pulled away from the TV but at the same time felt drawn to it. Now for the first time she understood what Jack's life was all about. The book. The torture. The scars on his back. *I wish I was there to hold him and keep him safe. How could she be so blind as to not understand what was going on in his life? Why did she not ask him more questions?*

"That had to be terrifying in itself, Dr. Petersen?"

"Yes it was Matt. They treated me in a field hospital for a broken arm and a concussion. Then a couple of days later I was blindfolded and driven away to some prison. I later learned I was being held at the notorious Evin Detention Compound which they called the People's Liberation Detention camp. It is where they keep their political prisoners in Tehran."

"Were you healed from your injuries by that time?" asked Susan.

"Not really. The first day I was at the prison, they took me from my cell to a small interrogation room. They sat me down in front of a small wooden desk, shoved a piece of paper in front of me and handed me a pen, saying *Sign it*. I refused.

"The warden, Hakem Ahoud, brought me some papers and told me they were my release papers. The papers were written in their native Farsi but not translated into English so I could read them. I asked for a translator and they hit me on my back with a long metal rebar rod. They kept hitting me and hitting me until I dropped the pen and refused to do anything."

Jack shifted in his chair, uneasy speaking about his ordeal, before he said, "The beatings began again this time with three guards beating my back every day, then my feet. I still have scars on my back from their beatings." He took a sip of water from his glass nearby. "The guards threw me into a cell about the size of a small closet."

Jack shook slightly. He was reliving his terrible ordeal, as the tears rolled down her cheeks.

"They repeated the same scene over and over. Once they tied me into the chair and the main interrogator said if I was not going to sign the papers I did not need my fingers and proceeded to break one of my fingers. Then another. They took ages to heal properly."

"But you were just a doctor? Why would they do those terrible things to you?"

"I was in a United States military uniform, and I crashed in their sovereign territory and they treated me as either a spy or a military combatant, depending on the day of the week. They hate Americans, they hate the military, and they hate spies. They viewed me as all three unfortunately."

"How did you cope for three years, Doc?"

"One day at a time, Matt. One day at a time."

Katie curled up next to Felix on her sofa and could see Jack's hands ever so slightly begin to tremble. Tears formed in the corner of her eyes, slowly dripping down her cheeks.

"What kept you going?"

"They found out I was doctor and brought me my physician's bag from the downed helicopter. They had no medical staff to take care of the prison inmates or the guards for that matter. I wanted desperately to stay in touch with my wife. I was afraid that as her disease would progress she would not remember me or our marriage or the times we shared. So, they bargained with me, if I would provide medical care for the inmates they would allow me the opportunity to write home to my wife. After three weeks I finally agreed when the warden son suffered from an illness." Jack took another sip of water.

"They decided they would allow me to write my wife one letter a month but I could not say how I was being treated, where I was being held, or by whom, otherwise my letters would be confiscated and destroyed. I could also not mention anything about anyone else. I could not mention my fellow prisoners, the guards or say anything about anyone, including my son Danny."

"They play by some pretty tough rules, don't they?"

"I broke the rules once and mentioned something about the guards in passing in one of my letters and they made me pay for my mistake. They apparently didn't censor it but the commander saw a photocopy of the letter after it was already sent and they didn't let me write home for three months."

"Very strange rules and you could usually write a letter once month?" interjected Susan, now suddenly focused and very interested in the man sitting before her when she heard the romantic elements creep into his conversation.

"Yes, that was it, one letter per month. At the beginning of the year they would bring me twelve pieces of paper and a pen. They were always different color paper, some blue, some yellow whatever they had around at the moment but the message was the same, one per month."

"Your wife must treasure those letters as something special," Susan said.

Katie leaned forward to listen to his response, when the phone rang.

"Put the TV on," Jessie started, before she got cut off by Katie.

"I know, I am watching it, I got to go," Katie said and hung up.

Felix purred behind Katie for attention and obtaining none, he climbed onto her lap, curling into a ball to make himself comfortable and fell asleep.

"Yes she did, I am told by my son, Danny."

"What, if you don't mind me asking, did you write in your letters to your wife?" Susan asked.

"I wanted to write to her, to try to help her in the only way that I could, to try to help keep her memory alive and active. I kept asking her to remember the things we did and places we had been, anything to help keep her memory of us alive." Jack stopped for a moment.

"I wrote to her about us. I wrote to her of things we did and places we visited and the many things we shared but without breaking their rules. I wanted her to remember us. That was the most important thing I could do with my life and I always asked her to remember everything we did and all that we shared. My son Danny now calls it my *Remember Philosophy*."

"That must have been hard."

"Yes indeed, it was very hard. I wanted to tell her everything. I could not be with her because I was being held hostage. I wanted to be there for her but I did not know when I would be freed. They would read my letters. If I put any information in them about my treatment or where I was they would destroy the letter and take away my privileges for another month. Sometimes if they got drunk or particularly angry they would break another of my fingers just for spite. But I could not take the chance of losing what little contact I had with my wife for another month. If the pen ran out of ink they would not replace it."

"Did they let your wife write to you, Dr. Petersen?"

"No, they didn't. But you see my wife was a writer, a poet really. She wrote poetry under the name Allison White. When she would receive one of my letters, my son, who was taking care of her told me, she would pen a poem in response and put it in a binder. My son later published the book of her poems."

"What was the name of her book of poems?" asked Matt.

"It was called, *Yearnings.*"

"How long were you a prisoner?" asked Matt.

"Almost three years."

"Did they continue to beat you?"

"Yes, but towards the end, only occasionally. They were wretched people. Sometimes they would grow bored with me and decide to amuse themselves by throwing me in solitary confinement. The only time I was let out is when I treated the prisoners and then they had me treating the guards. When I began treating the guards the behavior and the food got better. "

"How did it finally turn out, Dr. Petersen?" interjected Matt.

"I was exchanged for their spy Ahmed Taruk at a border crossing. They were happy to get rid of me when our State Department got wind that I was alive because of the letters and put pressure on the

Iranians. They were happy to have their number one spy back home in Tehran and I guess they had gotten all the mileage they could out of my capture."

"I guess your wife was pretty happy that you were coming home?" asked Susan as she leaned closer to hear his response.

For the first time Katie could tell Jack was really choked up and could not answer, until he said, "Well yes, I suppose she would have been, if she had lived. She died three months before I was released. I never knew she died. Those damn Iranians never told me, they just let me keep writing the letters to her so I would medically treat them. Maybe they never knew but I think otherwise."

"I am so sorry to hear that, Dr. Petersen. How did she die?"

"She died from pneumonia from a lung infection. It was an underlying result of Alzheimer's and her weakened immune system. I miss her so, even to this day."

"Do you have any of the letters you wrote to her? Did she keep them?" asked Susan.

"I no longer have the letters. They were either lost when I moved or they were just misplaced," he said, preferring not to go into any further details.

"I am sure you are sorry to hear that. They must have been very special. And you could not find them?"

"We never found them. After she died and I was released, we searched the house high and low and found none of the letters I had written. They were very special to me but they were nowhere to be found, I am sorry to say. I know of only one or two that has surfaced."

"I guess those letters in themselves would make another best seller, huh Doc?" asked Matt.

"Yes I guess so, but some things are so private, too private to even share with anyone, much less with the world in a book. They were written from my heart and soul and now they are gone."

Katie looked at the pile of letters stacked high on the buffet bound by a purple ribbon. They did not belong to her, they belonged to Jack. They always belonged to Jack and now she knew she could no longer keep them.

"How has your life been since you were released from captivity Dr. Petersen?"

"Well I've had my ups and downs. I met someone special since I lost my wife and I lost her too. I have loved two women in my life. I lost the first one to a terrible disease and lost the second one to terrible stupidity."

"Is that so? This new person in your life is she...?" Susan started to ask before she was interrupted by her partner Matt Mohr.

"So you are finishing your book tour, Dr. Petersen?"

"Yes, my last stop is next week in my hometown of Delray Beach Florida."

"Then what, Doc?"

"I plan to take some time off, drink some wine, fish and maybe write another book, maybe a book about my discoveries along the way of writing this first book."

"Thanks for coming in, Dr. Petersen. Please give a big round of applause to our special guest today, Dr. John Petersen author of *Captured*."

Katie looked at the large stack of letters, once so comforting now so foreign and she knew now what she had to do. God she missed him. She'd blown it big time.

• • •

Jack was back at his favorite Delray bookstore, Murder on The Beach. They were the first ones to carry his book and he never forgot that. It was a fitting place to end his nationwide book tour. The store was swarmed with people looking to buy the new up and coming bestseller from their hometown hero. They lined up around the block to have him sign their copy of the book. Women outnumbered the men two to one.

"How do I look?" Jack asked the manager.

"Good enough to eat, Doc," she said smiling. "Now go out there and wow them. And Doc..., you'll do just fine."

He signed copies of his book for over an hour, asking the same question, "Who should I make it out to and what do you want me to say?" Just before closing, the last book was placed before him and he asked the same question, "Who should I sign it to?" without looking up.

"Make it out to Katherine," responded a familiar voice.

"What should it say?"

"I would like to say, I'm sorry, Jack."

He looked up and saw Katie standing before him. He signed the book, and then handed it to her, without taking his eyes off her. She clung to the book when he had finished before placing a large stack of handwritten letters before him, bundled together with a purple ribbon.

"These are yours, Jack. They changed my life, my world. I'm sorry it took me so long to return them to you and I'm sorry for all the grief I may have caused you." She wanted him to have them and to have his private time.

"Thank you, Katie," he said, not taking his eyes off the treasure trove of letters before him.

Jack looked down at the multi-colored letters, so filled with emotion, so filled with love, as he touched them like the long lost manuscripts they were. The memories came flooding back to him. The years in captivity, the time separated from his family, the horrors he endured all came crashing over him. He could not help himself, filled with emotion, he began to cry. He slumped over the table, overwhelmed and continued to weep, tears of a long lost love, found. His journey was complete. He looked up to speak and console Katie, but she was gone. *Maybe she did not want to have anything more to do with him?*

Chapter Thirty-Five

Weeks later the art gallery opened at its usual time and all of the shoppers passed the book on display in the front window, it was Jack's book. Life had returned to normal for Katie, her paintings were drawing more acclaim than she ever could have imagined. She joined Jessie for lunch on a more regular basis and was starting to get on with her life.

"Have you heard from him since seeing him at the book signing?" Jessie asked.

"No."

"Do you want to talk about it?"

"No."

There was still an aching hole left in her heart which she did not know how to fill. Life was bearable, she would say, but really meaning tolerable, she missed Jack so much.

After lunch, on that sunny Thursday afternoon the mail was delivered and a large pile was placed on Katie's desk by her newest assistant, Ashley.

Jessie had taken a rare couple of days off to be with Mickie who was in town for two whole weeks. Jessie was in heaven. Their relationship was blossoming and he was even making sounds of settling down in Delray.

"I'm going for a latte, would you like one?" Ashley asked, nearly halfway out of her office.

"Sure, lots of sugar though. I like my coffee sweeter now for some reason."

Katie thumbed through the mail, bills, flyers, pizza promotions, until she held a white envelope addressed to her, written in a familiar handwriting. Her hand froze as she read the return address on envelope—Jack's beach house. She trembled, staring at it. He didn't move after all! He was still here. Her emotions were raw as she held his words in her hand, not knowing what he was about to say. She swallowed, opened the envelope and read his letter.

November, 2011

Dearest Katherine,

They say there is no greater fool than the one who thinks others to be foolish. I have found a light has been extinguished twice in my life and now wonder how I could ever let that happen. Such a fool am I. I sometimes feel I can express myself with pen and paper better than with spoken words.

I recall the life we were starting together, life filled with love, joy, tenderness and giving. Remember the time on the boat, our lovemaking to the sound of rain. Help me find the courage to chart our new course.

I can still feel your touch even though you are gone; the mere scent of a flower reminds me of the sweet smell of your perfume. I miss your touch. I miss your laugh, the crinkle of your nose when something strikes your funny bone. I yearn to hold you and never let you go. I am sorry to say I have lost my way, lost my compass to find you, to hold you, to need you. Emmis, my love.

Who am I to say that something is wrong, when I have made the greatest of errors and let this light slip so easily from my life? A new life which was just beginning for me, thanks to you. We were two new souls, both born of desperation and of love, clinging to one another and I walked away from that life. Forgive me; forgive my stupidity, if you can. I miss you and need you.

Forever,

Jack

Tears swelled in her eyes and she softly sobbed, not hearing Ashley enter her office and set down her coffee mug on her desk. Katie closed her office door and remained in her office for over an hour.

"I'll be back tomorrow," she said emerging from her office as she walked out the door.

"What?" said Ashley, astonished. "Who is going to close up, lock up and set the alarm?"

Katie turned to her. "You will Ashley. And if you don't get it right tonight you can try again tomorrow. Good night." She ran up the steps to change her clothes and grab some things before hustling off to her car.

She quickly drove down Atlantic Avenue, past all of the crowds and restaurants before making a left turn at the beach. She drove along A1A and watched as the sun set into an orange and red fireball, sinking on the horizon.

Katie pulled off the road into his long gravely driveway and parked her car, grabbing the picnic basket and blanket from the rear seat. She saw the house off to the side with a soft light on in the living room and walked up the steps by the dunes until she reached the top. It was then that she saw him.

She looked at him while he stood on the beach, in his ever present cutoffs and an old chambray shirt.

He cast the huge lure dangling at the end of his surf rod into a long spiral of line behind him, then snapped it forward into the frothy waves. A formation of sandy white and yellow beaked pelicans flew effortlessly overhead, gliding along the surfside, heading north along the coastline searching for fish.

Her spirits and heart soared as she approached him. Her heart pounded like she was racing to the finish line. She walked faster. Her mouth was dry as the salt air brushed her face.

"Hello Jack," she said quietly, walking up beside him.

He turned, the surf fishing rod still in his hand, to look at her. He smiled that wonderful smile of his and slid the rod into its beach holster.

"What a fool I have been," he started to say before she placed her finger to his lips, silencing him.

"That doesn't matter anymore. What matters is we are here. I have brought some wine and cheese," she said to him. "I thought we could sit here and talk and just be together."

"Yes, I would like that, I would like that very much," he said unable to take his eyes off her. He reached for her.

The electricity of their skin touching, holding one another again was beyond anything she imagined. She had missed his touch, his kiss and everything about him.

Katie found what she was looking for. And as they kissed, his arms encircling her, with the waves lapping at their ankles, Katie realized she had finally come home, home to his arms.

-The End-

Now an excerpt from Bryan Mooney's latest romance novel -

A SECOND CHANCE

By

Bryan Mooney

A Second Chance

Ravenna Morgan had it all. She was smart, attractive and well educated. After losing the love of her life she decided she had to get away from it all. Ravenna did what everyone would love to do…, she left and never looked back. She had a comfortable life on a small Greek island paradise nestled in the southern blue Aegean sea. It was filled with friendly people, beautiful beaches and warm sunny days. The strong willed woman thought she had left her life behind her… but she was wrong?

Now, torn between memories and guilt, she must decide- but will she get…a second chance?

Chapter One

Ravenna Morgan removed her robe and entered the quiet pool, naked; wearing only the thin gold chain and the dangling, gold Celtic cross she had worn since she was young. She swam with ease in the hotel's private lap pool, enjoying her daily, early morning swim.

Water glided over her body as she dipped her hands in front of her, crossing the pool with measured, elegant strokes. Her long red hair floated behind her. The soothing water massaged her athletic body and caressed her curves as she left gentle ripples in her wake.

She knew she could swim here, just outside her modest apartment, and not be disturbed. It was one of the few perks she truly enjoyed as resident manager of the Hotel Petros.

There was another pool for hotel guests in the front of the building. From there you could see for miles past the turquoise blue waters of the Aegean Sea. While it featured the most spectacular, panoramic views of the island and the waters beyond, her pool featured tree shrouded privacy.

The hotel was empty, which was common at this time of the season. The large private luxury yachts would come at the end of the month and stay to enjoy the beautiful beaches and her fabulous cooking. They would be making their Southern sojourn turn before heading back to the more populated Northern islands, like Mykonos. Here, they were far from all of the other islands, and she liked it that way.

When they came, the wealthy men would drool over the tall, shapely Irish beauty and even her gold wedding band did not stop them from making their usual advances. Sometimes it would take the presence of her better half, Trevor, to cool the hot passion of some of her more amorous visitors.

But by and large, most guests were gracious and appreciated the laid back atmosphere and lifestyle on the beautiful island of Petros. They came to enjoy the splendor of the crystal blue water for swimming and diving, along with the fine sandy beaches on the other side of the island. But most of them only wanted a long hot shower, a good meal, a full sized bed and the opportunity to listen to Ravenna strum her guitar and sing around the patio fireplace at night. Even life aboard a luxury yacht has its limitations and becomes tedious after a while.

On the tiny island there was no airport, no television, no cell phone service, no radio signals, and limited internet service. But the hotel offered plenty of peace and quiet high atop the hill and it was the quiet, laid back atmosphere that Ravenna loved.

Her regular visitors, after they left the island, would send her music and books. She loved cookbooks and travel books. The hotel had stacks of musical CD's sitting at the front desk outside the bar, sent from her guests as they made their journeys around the globe. She loved to listen to the music and she loved to dance. The one thing she did miss was the dancing more than anything else. Trevor no longer liked to dance, "Too tiring," he would always say.

When she finished her swim and toweled off, she showered, then dressed for a day in town. She pulled on her loose fitting Levi's cutoffs, slipped on her handmade leather sandals and tossed on an old Greek peasant blouse, which was cut low to reveal her ample female charms.

The tall striking beauty, with her emerald green eyes, young figure and morning glory smile, felt right at home on this slow paced island paradise. At age forty-four she could have easily passed for someone ten years younger. She was easy to pick out in a crowd and stood in stark contrast to the dark-haired island older resident women who always dressed in black. Her beauty even rivaled the younger female residents who with their flashing eyes, dark hair and mysterious good looks were some of the most beautiful women on earth.

She reread Trevor's note which he left on her bedside table and she found when she awoke that morning.

R-
I did not want to wake you.
Will be back in a week.
See you soon.
Trevor

Trevor and Mickel, the hotel's occasional fix-it man, had already left for the ferry. She hated to see him go even though it was only for a week. Dressed, she headed for the lobby of the small hotel.

Ravenna positioned the welcome sign on the registration counter. It directed those who found their way to the hotel to sign in and choose a room key and make themselves at home. Everything was very informal and relaxed at her island hotel hideaway. Hotel Petros was one of two hotels. The other hotel on the island was Zorbas, which catered to Greek visitors from the other side of the island.

Ravenna grabbed a flower from a pink trailing vine near the hotel's swinging entrance gates. She pinned the blossom behind her ear and took in a deep breath of fresh air.

She was always in awe of the view from her hilltop hotel. Far in the distance she could see the nearest islands, an hour away by fishing boat. She noticed the bustling village below and the shallow, light blue water that surrounded the island. From her hillside perch she gazed further out to sea at the calming azure Aegean water made noticeable by the dark blue shades as the water became deeper. It was a breathtaking sight. Down below was the harbor town of Thios.

As Ravenna made her way down the steep hill into town for her grocery shopping, the pretty Irish American lass hummed an old Irish tune, *Carrickfergus*. She loved the ancient Irish song she had learned as a child from her parents. She was born in Ireland, outside of the town of Limerick but moved with her family to Saint Louis when her father got a job with an American company.

The road down to the village of Thios was partially paved with irregular peanut sized rocks. The loose stones kicked out from under her sandals, sending them bouncing in front of her. She watched them roll down the dusty road.

She passed row upon row of brightly colored flowers, hanging from vines everywhere. Their colors harmonized with the colors of the rainbow. She sniffed the blooms of her favorite flowers including the lemon yellow claritis, dark purple bougainvilleas and the magnificently flavored hot pink passion flowers.

While some flowers clung to nearby fences, others sprouted from old stone pots and anywhere else these beautiful wild flowers could find an inch of ground. Flowers staked their claim to the overgrown telephone poles and dangled from telephone wires. Ironic she thought, the phone lines were good for something since it was next to impossible to make calls off the island. She loved the flowers and the sweets smells which always filled the air around her on the island.

She glanced around at the beautiful vistas and thought to herself, I love it here. She smiled. Maybe today would be a good day after all.

Her thoughts drifted back to her childhood in Saint Louis and the many friends she had left behind her so many years ago. She smiled as the thoughts caught her imagination and filled her with wonder. *I wonder what happened to them?* She walked towards the village, lost in her own thoughts, but soon her past would come rushing back to her and quicker than she ever would have imagined.

Chapter Two

"Come on you old slow poke, get a move on," shouted Gabi Branigan to her husband Jack, as she sprinted down the side street to the beach leading him by more than four lengths. She ran track in college and stayed in great shape all the years of their marriage.

"Okay, okay, I'll give you a race for your money," Jack responded. *One of these times, he would like to outrun her. Just once. She was very competitive and he was never able to beat her.* Jack stretched his long frame and pumped his legs to the max. He looked up; he was closing on her.

When she turned her head, she was shocked to see him gaining distance. She ran faster and pulled somewhat ahead. She was not going to lose to anyone not even her loving husband Jack.

He closed the distance and was soon neck and neck with his erstwhile opponent. One last push and then he passed her and made it to the beach four strides ahead. He had beaten her! For once in his life he had beaten his wife Gabi in a foot race. He would never let her live this down.

"I know, I know you were tired and out of shape. I understand," he said to her, huffing and puffing, still out of breath.

"You don't need to make any excuses for me." She smiled, with a pout beginning to grow on her lips, looking for sympathy despite her protests to the contrary.

He pulled her close and leaned forward to kiss her. He could feel her pressing into him, her heart still racing from their chase, her breasts firm as his lips neared hers. It was so good to see her smile again. He went to hold her closer, to kiss her…

WHOOOO!!!!… WHOOOO!!!!… WHOOOO!!!!…

The deep baritone sound of the Greek island ferry horn boomed loud overhead. It startled Jack from his sleep and in an instant his dream dissolved and she was gone.

The sound cracked the air and broke the silence on the rusting ship. It blasted a deep hello, announcing its presence, *WHOOOO!!!!… WHOOOO!!!!… WHOOOO!!!!…*

The sound was distant, as if it did not matter to him. He was tired and glad to be able to finally get some rest. It felt good just to lie there on the lower bunk bed on the slow moving inter-island ferry. He wondered if he tried real hard, could he pick up his dream where he left off? He had outraced Gabi! Probably not, he finally concluded. With half opened eyes, he surveyed his surroundings, then he remembered he remembered where he was—a small cabin onboard an old Greek ferry on his way to the island of Mykonos.

A cute, young booking agent in Piraeus persuaded him to upgrade to a "cabin suite" on the ferry. He was so tired he would have agreed to anything the pretty young thing talked him into. She smiled at him the entire time as he completed the necessary paperwork. *She probably made a nice commission on this upgrade.*

He just barely fit in his "upgraded" bunk bed. It was obviously made for much shorter passengers. Jack was different than most of the typical men on the ferryboat. Jack was tall, with broad shoulders, unruly sandy-colored hair, deep blue eyes, sported an easy smile and was handsome to a fault. He did not know how handsome he was but women seated in restaurants would always strain to watch him walk past, much to Gabi's chagrin.

Even though he hated traveling by ship, he decided it was worth the trouble to get to Mykonos early rather than stay in Athens. It turned out he was wrong. Jack hated boats, he hated small ones in particular but he had no choice except to take the ferry to reach his destination. He hated the water. The rolling of the boat in the choppy seas made him seasick. He dreaded big ships and could not wait for the ferryboat ride to be over.

The Greek airline strike had crippled all airline travel in this Mediterranean country. The strike forced him to resort to travel by ferry boat. He did not relish spending any more time in the overcrowded city of Athens. The strike had immobilized the city, filling every hotel room with stranded travelers. In the narrow roads of the capital, taxis jammed the streets, bringing traffic to a standstill. In the hot late June Athens sun, every restaurant had lines of patrons outside waiting to be seated.

Before he settled in his small cabin, he wiped every handle, door knob and surface he touched with his ever present cleansing anti-bacterial wipes. He brushed off the mattress of the bunk bed with his hand, to clear away any lingering foreign objects. His loving wife

Gabi always preached to him that you could never be too careful where germs and dirt were concerned.

He snubbed out his cigarette in the dirty Cinzano ashtray and vowed again he would quit smoking, soon. He brought three cartons of cigarettes with him from the States and when those were gone, he was going to quit. *Promise! Yes, he would quit, soon.* Gabi always detested the rank odor from his cigarette smoke.

Jack turned his sport coat inside out and used it as a pillow to try to finally get some sleep. He rolled over on the short bed dreaming of how he yearned and loved the quiet solitude of the luxury accommodations of a suite at the Prince Edward Hotel on Mykonos. They had stayed there five years earlier and loved it. It was clean and expensive but worth every penny. He smiled thinking of the hotel. It was like staying at an upscale New York resort. The hotel was new, with a hot showers and room service which served hamburgers. Yes, that's the ticket, he thought.

The cabin on the ferry he rented for the six hour journey to Mykonos was not much larger than a typical American style walk-in closet. It also shared many of the same smells. The air was stale, clammy and had other scents he cared not to think about. He turned over on the cabin's narrow bunk bed, trying to get comfortable after his twenty hour, three airline flight journey from Chicago, before he fell back to sleep.

The ship's horn sounded again and again. WHOOOO!!!! WHOOOO!!!! WHOOOO!!!! The noise caused him to sit up in the small bed and he struggled to the look out of the tiny porthole in his cabin. He could see the deep blue Aegean Sea in the distance and the crystal clear light blue water nearby the ship. The small island town was retreating in the distance.

He looked to the hills beyond the village. As an architect he admired the architectural simplicity of the windmills high atop the hills, functional in their design and yet graceful in action, spinning ever so slowly. Jack could feel himself already starting to relax and enjoy his two week hiatus. He only had to endure the final boat ride to his destination. He came to Greece ten days early for the annual family reunion, so he could just relax on the beach at the Prince Edward and begin writing his book. He would enjoy the peace and quiet of the islands and rest.

His normal travel schedule was horrendous, traveling the globe non-stop as the front man for his international design firm. After the family reunion on Mykonos, things should settle down he hoped. Then he was off to a two month assignment in Australia for his company.

He would travel to Australia as an architectural/engineering liaison with the U.S. and Australian governments on a project being built out in the Northern desert of Australia. Even the Aussies, who were used to the rugged outback, called the building site the "boonies." Luckily he would be working in the city of Sydney in a comfortable air-conditioned office, soaking up Australian hospitality for two months. What a life, he thought, but it was getting old. He lay back down.

The old ferry's horn boomed again, rousing him, and shook the old boat to its sixty-year old core. WHOOOO!!!! WHOOOO!!!!

Jack froze. *Oh my God!* Panic set in. The boat was leaving the pier, he had overslept! *The windmills! The white buildings! The blue doors! He was at Mykonos! This was his stop!*

The inter-island ferryboat pulled away from the dock. Jack panicked, grabbed his bags, jacket, sunglasses, cigarettes, cell phone and his book from the small bedside table and made a mad dash for the gangplank. He ran down the narrow passageway, already over-crowded with passengers heading to other islands.

"Mykonos?" he asked an old woman dressed in black, standing in the hallway." Is this the island of Mykonos?"

"Mykonos," she responded and smiled a toothy grin. *Did she understand what I was asking* ?Jack thought to himself as the heard the horn again bellow overhead,

He ran as fast as he could manage, slipping on the old greasy passageway nearly tripping over a man in a wheelchair who was blocking his way.

"Sorry," he said, without pausing to look back.

"Hoy, no problem mate," came the understanding response from the man.

WHOOOOO!!!! The horn blared again. He could see them throwing off the ropes from shore and the ship pulling away from the old dock. Jack would have to jump for it. He strapped one bag over his head and shoulders and threw another ashore. It landed squarely on the old wooden pier. He threw his next bag. It hit the dock, bounced off and splashed into the murky waters churned up by the propellers of the rusty old ferry. He looked down as the leather bag floated by before disappearing into the waters below. His cigarettes were in that bag. No time to dwell on it now, he thought.

He leapt to the pier, landed, teetered on the edge but made a safe landing.

The horn blasted a final time, saying farewell.

Jack waved goodbye and good riddance to the old ferryboat. He turned and watched it chug away to the next island, leaving the dock behind. Jack scoured the nearby waters for evidence of his drowning bag, but it was gone. Well at least he'd made it. He walked down the long pier towards the town, pulling his luggage behind him. The roll-on luggage made a clunk, clunk, clunk noise as the hard plastic wheels hit the spaces between the boards on the old wooden pier.

The island looked smaller than he remembered as he clunked down the long dock. Mykonos was his wife Gabriella's favorite Greek island. That is probably why her sister, Joanie, suggested it for this year's family reunion, knowing that he would never object to such a choice. Well at least it was better than last year's choice of Boise, Sarah's hometown. Next year was his turn and his choice was going to be Sicily, where Gabriella's parents were born. They could stay at The Sicilian Grand Resort Hotel. He smiled to himself.

The tall American could feel the warmth of the island sun on his face. The breeze off the water cooled the afternoon heat. It felt good. He and Gabi always loved the Greek islands and visited them often. But now because of his constant travelling, he preferred the bigger islands with their newer hotels. They were clean, efficient and had twenty-four hour room service. Just like being at home.

As he made his way to the end of the pier, he was approached by a group of young boys, all in sandals, t-shirts, with dark tan faces, coal black hair with brilliant white, flashing smiles.

"American? Canadian? You need bed? Place for stay? Food?" peppered the tallest one and the apparent leader of the rag-tag group.

"American," he replied looking past them to the end of the pier.

"T-shirt? You like?" interrupted the smallest one, pushing in front of the group to sell his wares. He held up a t-shirt with the ubiquitous blue and white flag of Greece emblazoned on the front. He was soon pushed aside by the leader.

"I Stavros," he told the weary American. "My uncle, Nicolai, he own hotel downtown, Zorbas. You follow me. You like, I guarantee." The tall lad made an attempt to grab Jack's bag and lead him down the small main street to his uncle's hotel.

"No, thank you. I am with a group of other family members. I'm looking for the Prince Edward Hotel. Can you tell me how to find it? I have a reservation there."

"Prince Edward Hotel?" mocked the tall one named Stavros. His smile turned to a snicker.

"Yes, I'm looking for The Prince Edward," Jack repeated, weary from his long trip.

Stavros said something indiscernible in Greek to the assembled group of young friends. When he finished speaking, they all laughed and then began to point at him, laughing all the while.

"What is so funny," Jack asked. The boys reached the end of the pier and the group parted to allow Jack to read the blue and white sign which proudly proclaimed in three languages:

WELCOME TO THE ISLAND OF PETROS.

Petros? What the hell? No! It can't be, he thought to himself.

Jack had gotten off on the wrong island. Now what was he going to do? The town looked so small. They probably don't even have hot running water here. He'd have a glass a wine in town and wait for the next ferry. It couldn't be that long of a wait.

"When is the next ferry to Mykonos?" he asked the tall one.

"No ferries for another week, my American friend. Next Friday. Welcome to Petros! Enjoy your stay. See you in town at my uncle's hotel. Goodbye my American friend."

Jack stopped and watched them walk away. *What more could happen?…*

A Second Chance is available wherever fine books are sold.

CPSIA information can be obtained at www.ICGtesting.com
Printed in the USA
LVOW101136240313

325749LV00014B/604/P